GALWAY
CONFIDENTIAL

GALWAY CONFIDENTIAL

A JACK TAYLOR MYSTERY

KEN BRUEN

THE MYSTERIOUS PRESS
NEW YORK

GALWAY CONFIDENTIAL

Mysterious Press
An Imprint of Penzler Publishers
58 Warren Street
New York, N.Y. 10007

Copyright © 2024 by Ken Bruen

First Mysterious Press edition

Interior design by Maria Fernandez

Library of Congress Control Number: 2023918646

ISBN: 978-1-61316-479-2
eBook ISBN: 978-1-61316-480-8

10 9 8 7 6 5 4 3 2 1

Printed in the United States of America
Distributed by W. W. Norton & Company

For

Dr. Charlie Cox

Lifesaver

Sheila Winston

A wonderful reader

"If you do
What you always did,
You'll get
What you always got."
—Declan Coyle
The Green Platform

The man looked down at the woman. His third fist to her head
had knocked her unconscious; he briefly considered killing her
but moved back, whispered,

"Not yet."

He gathered up his kit,

> Rope,
>
> Duct tape,
>
> Handcuffs,
>
> Knife,
>
> And a recent addition to his trade,
>
> > A mountaineering hammer
> >
> > that
> >
> > doubled as an axe.

He hefted it in his hand, thought,

"I could take her head."

Stood back and laughed out loud, said,

"Just kidding, these are the jokes."

He reached in his backpack, took out a pack of Marlboro
Red, the soft pack you rarely saw anymore, shook one out

like they do in the movies, lit it with a heavy Zippo that had the logo:

"C

Is

For

Cun . . ."

Tickled him each time.

He let the ash grow on the tip then, with a definite gesture, flicked it on the supine woman, said,

"Ashes to ashes."

Gathered up his gear, took one last look around, then let himself out through the ground-floor window.

The nun on the ground groaned quietly but remained unconscious.

C

is

for

Confidential

Control

Calibre

Contempt

Cri de Coeur

Covetous

Courage

Catastrophe

C is thus a multifaceted letter, but for the man who attacked nuns, it filled his head with one of his bon mots:

Chaos

1

How do you come out of a coma?

Really
    Really
        Slowly.

Or—
So they told me.

I opened my eyes after what seemed like an ice-white light had filled my head.

Hospital.

Tubes stuck in/attached to every orifice.

I was bewildered, befuddled, but mostly I was very—

Thirsty.

Like a bastard.

Moving very cautiously, I tried to sit up, kind of managed it. A man was sitting by my bed, wearing a surgical mask, serious save the cartoon characters sprinkled on it. He asked,

"Water?"

I nodded.

He stood, got a glass, filled it, then brought it to my mouth.

Nirvana.

I gulped it, coughed.

"Easy, easy big guy."

I tried to talk but my vocal cords felt mangled, atrophied.

More water.

I could feel something almost snap in my throat and prayed to some God that my speech was okay. Take speech from an Irish guy?

Just shoot him.

The man was in his fifties, dressed in a black tracksuit with gold trim on the side; it was expensive, I know that as the cheap version hung in my wardrobe, unworn and unloved. I'd been very drunk when I bought it.

Ah, glory days.

"Who are you?" I asked, my voice fighting to return.

He sat back down, intoned, "*Mise Raifteirí an file / Lán dúchais is grádh.*" (I am Raftery, a poet / Full of hope and love.)

Paused, made a flourish with his hand, a gold claddagh ring glinting in weak Galway sun from the bay window and almost

involuntarily I volunteered, *"Le súile gan solas / Le ciúnas gan crá."*
(With eyes without light / Calm without anguish.)

◾

We'd recited that in primary school, so embedded that I could recall
the lines without trouble. The memory was accompanied by the lash
of bamboo across my knuckles. Inflicted by the brothers of mercy, to
whom mercy was an alien concept, maybe even, God forbid, Protestant.

A daze of corporal punishment colored all my schooling.

You got walloped, suck it up.

Raftery was a Medieval blind poet who traveled the countryside, poetry
for substance. Nowadays he'd get a medical card and direct provision.

Raftery, the present one, explained, "I can trace lineage back to the
blind bastard, so Raftery is the moniker I trade under."

He reached in a holdall by his feet, produced a hip flask with leather
trim, asked, *"Uisce Beatha?"* (Water of Life?)

This translates as *holy water*, but in Ireland means moonshine/
poitín.

Coming out of a coma of nigh two years duration, is booze the
way to go?

Fucking A.

I nodded so he held my head back, tilted the flask, and I drank.

Wow.

Phew-oh.

It kicked like a Connemara pony.

Brief interlude as my ravaged system tried to assimilate this ferocious insult, and then—

Bliss.

Utter.

I relaxed, sank back into the pillows with a deep sigh of contentment. Whatever shenanigans had landed me in a coma, in the hospital, ebbed away like the dying light of evening devotion.

Raftery asked in mock FBI tone,

"You'll be wanting data?"

Not really.

Another shot from the flask and I might never question anything again, ever.

A doctor, trailed by a coven of nurses, came rolling in.

"Mr. Taylor, you're back."

He sniffed, took a moment, then snarled,

"Who's drinking?"

Glaring at Raftery, who smiled weakly, the doctor said,

"It would be beyond madness to give a revived patient alcohol."

Then he and the nurses began a series of tests, prods, blood samples, and all the other paraphernalia designed to keep the patient in a state of imminent terror.

Raftery shunted from the room, gave me a wave.

"We'll talk soon, Jack."

The doctor said,

"We have to remove the feeding tube and it may be a tad uncomfortable."

Taking the tube from my stomach, I'd like to say I took it like a man.

No.

I howled like a bastard.

The doctor, finally finished with manhandling me, stood back, hands on his hips, dismay writ large on his face.

"Mr. Taylor, you're a mystery, one might even hazard a miracle, but you're in good health, which is just amazing."

I gave him a smile of what I thought might be appreciation but more likely transformed into a grimace.

I don't do appreciation.

He then outlined a program of therapy and rehabilitation.

"After which you're free to go."

Then, muttering, he left, literally scratching his head.

I looked to the least severe nurse, echoed,

"Therapy!"

Nora declared her name badge.

"Jack, you've been in a coma for eighteen months, it takes time to get the body up and functioning, to get you . . ."

Searched for a word.

"Mobile."

Confidential
Is the excuse
Sometimes used
Not to reveal
A dirty secret.

2

Two months of grueling PT nearly dissipated what little spirit I had, but slowly, very slowly, I began to function.

Nora was my coach, as it were, and she never cut me any slack, and like the Galway Girl she was, she had some mouth on her. Any attempt at sympathy was blown out of the water.

Worse, she seemed to find me amusing. Few things are more devastating that a girl mocking you. She was about 5'7", jet-black hair, a nose that, alas, slanted to the right, thus spoiling the shot at pretty.

During one of the rare breaks she allowed, she told me she was a boxer, added,

"So, don't fuck around with me Taylor."

As if!

I did venture,

"Why boxing?"

I didn't really care but it was something.

Got the look, the one that screams,

Where the fuck you been?

I nearly said,

"In a coma, actually."

Or, as a Galway wit called it,

"A comma."

Pause.

"Don't come to a full stop."

Galway banter.

Still, each day, I got a little stronger.

Nora, believing I was interested, said, "Women's boxing got a huge boost when Kelli took gold at the Olympics."

Kelli?

I didn't ask so much as devour and assimilate the internet for two years of events.

Sports.

Life.

Politics.

Television.

The public had to observe a two-meter distance because of Covid.

The two-meter distance didn't make a whole lot of difference as I had spent my life swerving away from folk.

And handshaking—my hands usually shook so I had mostly avoided touching other's hands. The wearing of masks creeped me out.

My mind veered between snapshots of the attack that put me there and this harsh new reality. Mostly I felt—not panic attacks, but being petrified.

Some days I could absorb huge chunks of data and others—

Nowt.

My first unsupervised shower, I finally looked at my torso, the knife scars.

Red, still raw in appearance. I felt dizzy and the room spun. I muttered,

"Get a grip, get a fucking grip."

How the hell did I survive it?

Well, part of me didn't, never would.

The words of the doctor ringing in my ears,

"How on earth did you live?"

I said bitterly,

"Just freaking lucky."

I noticed Nora had a large rock on her finger, an engagement ring, I said,

"Hell of a stone."

She gave a spontaneous laugh, and oh Lord, how it transformed her face, the eyes lit with joy. Joy is not something I've had much depth in. I pressed,

"Who's the guy?"

Paused, added,

"Sorry, these days I believe it is significant other or some such shite. A doctor, I suppose?"

She literally . . .

Tut-tutted . . .

Said,

"A doctor? God save us."

Looked at me, wondering how much was safe to tell me, then,

"Colin is a Guard. You know, the Garda, like a cop?"

I went quiet, regrouped,

"I know the Guards."

Her face clouded briefly; I might even have detected a hint of sadness. She said,

"I know."

To end the chat, she closed the topic by taking my blood pressure, gave that *uh-huh* that tells you zilch.

Means you'll never see Christmas, or worse, it's already the festive season.

One thing I'd learned since coming back (that's how I saw it, I'd come back) was keep the medical questions to the basics, fewer frights that way.

I did some deep breathing, and she was obviously pondering a thought, then,

"Colin says you're a legend."

I laughed, said,

"Legendary fuckup."

She nodded and I thought she might have at least tried to mitigate the image.

I eased myself into the bedside chair, the PE had been especially rough that day, and saw copies of *The Irish Independent* on my table.

"Your brother brings them in."

"Tell him I'm more of a Joycean." (As if.)

Got a lovely smile from her; she said,

"What you are is a bit of a divil" [*sic*].

She looked at me, added,

"But he's not your brother."

Bold statement.

"How'd you know, I mean he could have been."

She sighed.

"The day after you were admitted, he showed up, said he was"—she made air quotes—"'family,' but he seemed sketchy on personal details, and I just didn't like him."

Then she added as an afterthought,

"He doesn't look anything like you."

She fluffed up my pillows, gave me a long look, cautioned, said,

"Don't believe most of what he says, he has the cut of a liar."

I thought about my last case, just before I got attacked.

My friend, a garrulous Scot and intuitive Falconer, had a farm outside town and staying with him was a young lady.

My friend, the girl, the horses, all had been massacred in a situation nobody saw coming.

Some time later, his lawyer/accountant got in touch telling me that he's left me the farm and a stash of cash.

Weird, right?

He bought the farm.

I inherited it.

Giraldus Cambrensis wrote that,

"Ireland was separated from the rest of the known world,

And

In some sort to be distinguished

As another world."

3

A café in Woodquay was advertising:

> Couscous
>
> And
>
> Crubeens

Couscous is, of course, Moroccan grain and crubeens are pigs' feet.
How far the country had progressed in so many forms.

In my childhood we had:

Bacon

Cabbage

Spuds

I haven't advanced a whole lot in dietary terms.

The brief new trend of eating out was blocked by the lockdown and
the rain. Trotters were regarded as poor food even in terms of pov-
erty and to be bought in Quay Street.

Quay Street was then a shabby line of pawnshops and dodgy cafés. A man could pawn his suit on a Sunday and then redeem it on payday before a weekend of drink.

Who knew Quay would become a trendy nightspot and then later metamorphose to being The Latin Quarter?

None of the locals ever called it that, no matter how many signs they put up. You'd be hard put to find a crubeen in The Latin Quarter, but couscous, buckets of it.

I had my mental faculties tested by a young female psychiatrist named Dr. Lydon. She looked a little like Noirin, who worked alongside Vinny in Charlie Byrne's bookstore. My memory must have been okay since I remembered those two people. She was all eagerness and bubbling with inexperience.

She was overfond of terms like,

Empathy,

Owning my feelings,

Admitting my anger.

She finally finished up that spiel, asked,

"How are we today?"

Uh-huh.

"Dunno about you, Doc, but I'd kill for a cigarette and two shots of Jay."

She echoed,

"Jay?"

Lord on a bike.

"Jameson, what we Catholics drink."

She gave an audible,

"Ah."

Scribbled furiously in her notes, you could almost hear her think,

"Breakthrough."

All gung ho, now she asked,

"Would you classify your drinking . . ."

Pause.

Reached for a non-alarmist term, settled with,

"Problematic?"

I surprised her by almost on the trot replying,

"Most definitely."

Plead guilty and you disarm them instantly. I looked at my bare wrist, no watch, said,

"I think we've got through enough for today and I am pleased at your progress, we're in good shape."

Her face registered surprise and I felt a bit guilty, but what the hell, she was getting the big bucks.

I stood up, ended with,

"Same time next week and keep taking the meds."

Covid-19 had killed five thousand people. An unaccountable number were hospitalized, ICU had literally run out of beds due to the sheer volume of cases.

But.

Nigh on 90 percent of the population had received the two doses of the vaccine.

But.

The pubs had now been closed for eighteen months. Eighteen dry fucking months. The lockdowns had almost killed the bar trade completely. Shebeens sprang up but the Guards were on the prowl and shut them down.

Woe is me.

The heroes of the virus were the frontline workers who were exposed firsthand to the plague and went about their vital work in a quiet, dignified fashion.

True grit.

I was reading the paper; Ronaldo had returned to Man United after sixteen years and for his very first game he scored two goals. The man was a magician.

Nora appeared, said,

"Your brother is here."

She didn't believe he was related but seemed happy enough to go along with the charade.

Raftery was dressed in a tan safari jacket. He didn't have a cravat, but the intention was there. He had dark jeans, with a tear at the knee, as was fashionable. He had Doc Martens with, I suspect, a metal toe cap.

Apart from the jacket, it was the gear I wore my own self but any tear in my jeans was from age. Nora breezed in, shot a dark look at him, fluffed my pillows as they do, then bounced off.

Raftery moaned,

"She doesn't love me."

His tone suggested,

"What's not to love?"

"She hates liars."

He faltered then rallied, said defiantly,

"The whole brother ruse was the only way to get to see you."

I near shouted,

"But who the fuck are you?"

He tapped his pockets, said,

"Ah, for a smoke, eh?"

Continued,

"It was pure chance I was coming along the bridge when I saw the guy knifing you."

He stopped and I made the gesture with my hand that says,

"And?"

He seemed to zone, then snapped back, looked at me in confusion, then,

"Ah, details. What happened next was the purest simplicity."

Another long pause, until,

"I picked him up and flung him over the bridge."

He sighed, continued,

"Unfortunately, some do-gooder pulled him out. The Guards arrived and they took him away. He's been on remand ever since. I guess they were waiting to see if you'd die so they could charge him with murder."

I said,

"Sorry to have spoiled the party."

He waved his hand, no biggie, took out his flask, drank deep, went,

"Ah!"

Then offered.

I took it with joy, took a huge wallop. Almost instantly my stomach warmed, the world brightened, a free-floating anxiety evaporated.

I asked Raftery,

"Who are you?"

He gave a long sigh, began,

"You think an ordinary joe would be able to disarm a man with a knife then pick him up and throw him over a bridge? No. I have dual nationality, Irish and American. I spent time as a US Marine, moved fast through the ranks as I had the three things they respect:

"Lack of empathy.

"Hardcore toughness.

"Ruthlessness.

"I had a buddy, let's call him Quinlan, and we were tight, bonded by war.

"After we left the service, we ended up in London and he betrayed me, over fucking money. When I saved you, Jack, you became my new buddy, a replacement for that rat."

Nora came bustling in, snarled,

"Happy hour?"

Raftery gave her a long appraisal, asked,

"How are you not married?"

I was out of hospital, my physical recovery had been good, astounding, according to the doctor.

My mental well-being was, well, fucked. The world was so utterly altered that I couldn't get a grip.

The pubs were reopened, kind of. Sets of regulations made it nigh impossible to know what the hell was acceptable.

You could order a pint but not drink it at the counter. Distance between tables was damn confusing and the two-meter distance between people was just ridiculous.

The three lockdowns hadn't full killed the pub trade, but it had sure delivered a brutal assault.

The masks?

Shoot me now.

Took me days/daze before I could wear one correctly. I had it upside down, inside out, and it made my nose run from the sheer dryness of my nostrils.

Having a pint, you could de-mask and then re-mask when not drinking. Most of the public had grown accustomed to all the ever-changing rules.

I had a way to go.

I was in Garavan's, working on a second pint, between masks. A Jay was riding point. I liked how the weak winter sun cut through the gold liquid, giving it a sheen of hope.

Raftery arrived, wearing a Hugo Boss jacket, I know as it said so on the sleeve. He had tan cords over very polished brogues, white shirt, and a tie; the tie was loosely fastened to declare,

I'm square but cool with it.

He clapped me on the back, never a smart move as arms had been broken over such unwanted gestures. He asked,

"Did you hear about Trump's son?"

I hadn't.

Raftery said,

"He's selling T-shirts with the logo:

"'Guns don't kill people

"'Alec Baldwin does.'"

I shook my head, the sheer nastiness of that was incomprehensible.

Raftery ordered a coffee, asked if I wanted a pint. I didn't, trying to pace myself. He said,

"The country is short of clowns!"

This was too easy and too many quips were available, so I went with,

"What?"

He made a mock gesture of blessing himself.

"Cross my heart. Duffy's circus lost their crew during lockdown and can't now entice them back. There is also a shortage of lorry drivers and a blockade stemming from Brexit."

I asked,

"Where did the clowns go?"

Raftery just smiled.

He had been a staple in my life since my discharge from hospital. Truth be told, he was mostly an annoying bollocks, but I was glad of a guide through this new convoluted existence.

He slurped his coffee, few sounds as irritating; he caught the look on my face.

"What's eating you, bro?"

Bro!

I sighed. I come from a long line of sighers. My mother, the bad bitch, could have sighed for Ireland. Irish men are supposed to love their mammies.

Phew-oh.

Not me, not ever. She was the walking shape of pure malignancy, and pious to boot.

Before I could answer Raftery, a woman pushed through the drinkers, heading for me.

Raftery said,

"Your ship might be coming in."

There was never a cliché that Raftery could resist. The woman was in her early fifties, if age can be gauged anymore, the lockdowns had aged everybody. She was dressed in a black wool coat with face mask to match, much like a bird of ill omen.

Prophetic, as it turned out.

She had a riot of brown curls and a face completely unlined; it was her eyes that spoke of age. My mind suggested,

"Nun."

She asked of us both,

"Mr. Jack Taylor?"

Mister!

I nodded,

"Call me Jack."

She looked like she might shake hands but that was outlawed with the Covid regulations. People compensated with elbow touch and the cool kids did knuckle knock.

"I'm Sheila Winston."

Pause.

With a touch of apology, she added,

"I used to be a nun."

I offered,

"A drink?"

She shook her head,

"Might I have a word in private?"

Sensing my reluctance, she said,

"Sister Maeve was my friend."

Felt the stab in my heart. Maeve was my friend for years, the nun and the alkie, what a concept. I had been the cause of her death and her death haunts me always.

Seeing my distress, Sheila rushed on,

"I'm so sorry, I didn't mean to dredge up sorrow."

I shook myself,

"There's a quiet corner over there by the window, we can talk there."

As we moved in that direction, Raftery winked at her.

We settled ourselves at a small table. I said,

"What's the problem?"

"Maeve used to talk about the help you sometimes lent the church."

"Believe you me, it wasn't a big deal, but it brought a ton of trouble in its wake and I'm out of the helping sector, I barely survived my last outing."

She nodded.

"I heard about the attack on you, but if I may, you look much recovered."

I said,

"I'm getting there, slowly, so you'll understand I'm not much use to anybody else."

She considered this, then,

"Nuns are being attacked."

A showstopper.

I said,

"Go to the Guards."

"I've been but they are nigh overwhelmed with the demonstrations against the lockdowns and, too, assaults from the anti-vaxxers."

I tried to show some interest,

"How many nuns have been attacked?"

"Two, but the second assault was more vicious, as if the perpetrator is building in ferocity. I'm fearful he's building up to an actual killing."

Made a horrible sense.

I had to ask the delicate question,

"Is there, erm, a sexual element to the attacks?"

She blushed.

Who blushes anymore?

She shook her head. I asked,

"Do you want me to talk to the nuns?"

She was horrified.

"Oh no, they'd never be able for that."

I was relieved but how could I even begin?

Before I could voice that, she reached in her bag, produced an envelope, said,

"It's not much, but I'll be able to get more."

I didn't take the envelope.

"Let me see what I can find out, then we can revisit fees."

"God bless you."

She gushed.

I figured somebody needed to.

She asked,

"Have you heard of Edge?"

I hadn't.

She went,

"It's supposed to be a small, organized group of people who administer justice when the law fails."

I spoke,

"Why are you not using them?"

She spoke,

"I found a contact for them but they turned me down. It seems they stay away from religious affairs."

4

Seven years ago, the horror of the mother-and-baby home was discovered by amateur historian Catherine Corless. She tracked down the death certificates for 796 babies who had died in the care of the Bon Secours nuns.

She then discovered that only three of the number had been buried in local cemeteries.

It emerged that the worst scenario was true.

The remains had been dumped into the chambers of an old septic tank.

The nuns had tried to sell the story that they were remains from the Famine but that was proved to be a complete fabrication.

The minister for children, four years ago, had promised a full excavation of the site.

Guess what?

Didn't happen.

The UN issued a stinging rebuke to the Irish government.

The infant mortality rate in the care home was off the scales: 802 children died in the home right up to 1961.

Clusters of death certificates showed many babies dying within weeks of one another.

Worse, most of the babies died of malnutrition.

The Bon Secours sisters describe themselves as a nursing congregation.

Further research showed some of the babies who didn't die were shipped off to American families. In return for a donation.

The Bon Secours order is a billion-dollar business with hospitals in the US and Ireland. They employ sixty thousand people.

They have offered two million euros toward the cost of exhuming the babies, whereas the cost of the operation will be at least thirteen million.

It is little wonder that nuns are fearful of being out in public.

Sister Agnes and Sister Mary were the names of the two nuns who had been attacked. They belonged to the Sisters of Mercy. I wanted to talk to them, but Sheila said that was out of the question.

They had been attacked in the early evening, two weeks apart. Sheila was convinced that a third attack was imminent. I was furious.

"You ask for help but where on earth am I supposed to begin?"

She gave me a long look, then,

"You are supposed to be good at this."

I told her in all truth,

"I was never good at it. I got lucky a few times and most of the cases got solved despite me, not because of me."

"You have a very dim view of yourself."

I said,

"You have no idea."

5

Sister Mary

Was the first victim.

She was only twenty-four and worked as a teacher in the city center. Returning to pick up essays, she had been waylaid at the rear of the school. A man appeared as if out of nowhere and punched her twice in the face, then hit her with a hammer/axe.

That she didn't die was a miracle.

She was in a coma, and I sure could identify with that. I did the old Guard gig of calling round to houses in the neighborhood, looking for CCTV, and discovered nothing.

Raftery volunteered to do part of the neighborhood but came up empty too. He said,

"This guy is a ghost. Either he's extremely lucky or very calculating."

I met with Sheila, told her I'd achieved nothing.

"Oh please, don't give up."

I was on the verge but said,

"I'll give it a few more days."

***

The second nun was Sister Agnes. She worked at the hospital and was returning to the convent when the man attacked her. Same MO, the punch to the face and then the hammer to the head. Raftery and I canvassed the hospital, surrounding houses, streets, CCTV, and again, nothing.

Raftery asked,

"You know what this means?"

When I shook my head, he said,

"We wait for the next attack and hope he slips up."

***

A fourth strain of the virus was causing the number of infected to sky-rocket and the government hinted at another lockdown. Nightclubs, which were just a month reopened, were now told they had to close at midnight, which was the time most clubbers went out!

The hospitals were on the cusp of total collapse. The frontline workers were beyond exhaustion. Dark days indeed.

Raftery said to me,

"You missed eighteen months of lockdown so now you might get to experience what it was like."

Sister Brid was horrified by the attacks on the two nuns. She knew them only slightly. She wondered what kind of person could inflict such injury. Passing the Cathedral, she considered going in and lighting candles for the sisters, but the Mother Superior had warned her flock,

Don't walk alone.

Don't linger after dark.

Brid glanced at the sky, thought it was still bright, and decided to fast-track the candles. Once inside she was glad the church hadn't yet gone electric, the whole ritual of getting a taper, lighting it, bringing it to the candles, gave her a sense of piety she rarely experienced.

She whispered to herself,

"Old school."

And smiled.

She didn't notice a lone figure enter from the rear and slip silently along the pews like a shark sensing blood.

6

The Mother Superior was having a frustrating morning. The pipes had burst, flooding a large part of the convent. Trying to get a plumber was testing her limited patience. The plumber said,

"If I come today, it's double rate."

She bit down on her lip.

"Why?"

He said,

"See, Sister, I had another job lined up."

Pause.

"A highly lucrative gig but I cancelled it to agree to help you."

She didn't believe a word of it, took a deep breath, said,

"Very well, what time might we expect you?"

He sighed, said,

"I'm running late but I should get there round three."

She wanted to scream but held it in.

"We'll see you then."

He said,

"I'll want paying up front."

She was outraged.

"That's a little out of the usual way of business."

He gave a nasty chuckle.

"I've been stiffed by the clergy before. One chancer told me he'd pray for me."

The Mother Superior thought,

You won't be in my prayers.

Asked,

"Might I inquire the cost?"

He reeled off the figure and she said,

"That's very steep."

There was bitterness in his voice when he spoke.

"The price of doing business, Sister."

And clicked off.

She was just drawing breath when the phone shrilled again. She grabbed it, said tersely,

"Yes?"

A man's voice.

"Whoa, not a very nunny opening."

Something in his tone put her in mind of slithery things. She asked,

"Who is this?"

He hummed the opening bars of "Sympathy for the Devil" by the Rolling Stones. Then said,

"Allow me to introduce myself."

Pause.

"How is your flock doing? Missing three, I daresay?"

She felt a kick to the stomach, tried,

"Is this some macabre joke?"

He snickered, said,

"Depends on who is laughing; are you laughing, babe?"

She thought she might throw up but managed,

"Who are you?"

A beat.

Then,

"Think of a number."

"What?"

"A number, Sister, give me a digit or I'll bring the wrath of hell to your door."

Without even thinking she said,

"Six."

Why on earth she said that she would agonize over through the years.

The man said,

"Good choice, leaves us with three to go, and I think that's doable, yeah?"

In desperation she begged,

"Who are you and what are these numbers?"

He laughed.

"Nuns. Three down and three to wallop."

She muttered,

"Sweet Lord in heaven."

The man said,

"God has left the building, or, rather, the convent."

She made a last-ditch effort.

"Come to the convent, we can talk, and maybe I can help you."

He snarled,

"Help? From a nun? Get real, Sister. I must go wash my hammer. It got messed up on the last outing. I used to use the axe but the hammer makes more of, how shall I put it, a crunch."

And he was gone.

The Mother Superior doubled over and managed to make it to the sink before throwing up. Her legs trembled and her heart pounded.

After a bit, she allowed herself a small sherry, well, a large one in a small glass, then tried to compose herself; the sherry was sweet and lit her empty stomach like burning coal. The tremors eased in her body, and she was able to make a call.

To Sheila Winston.

She said,

"Sheila, we may need that private investigator of yours after all."

7

During a previous case involving the church, I met a young priest named Father Pat. He was as raw a youth as you could find, but some time in my company and he developed a line in cynicism. His world view darkened.

Plus, he got a taste for Jameson and that is its own path to weariness.

I was in my apartment; it had been kept functional by Raftery while I was out of the game.

I was reading

The Wreck of the Deutschland

by Gerard Manley Hopkins.

It seemed appropriate as I read about the nuns drowning in the poem.

> *Sister, a sister calling*
> *A master, her master and mine!—*

And the inboard seas run swirling and hawling;
The rash smart sloggering brine

Raftery had gifted me a Nespresso and, wow, did that make seriously great coffee. I was on my second cup when the doorbell rang. Figuring it was Raftery, I opened the door.

Father Pat.

He looked kind of fucked.

No priest suit but it was not uncommon now for the clergy to keep a low, very low, profile. He was wearing a ragged sweatshirt with the logo *sweet meat.*

Cute.

He had blue jeans with a hole on the knee, less fashion than life. And a battered pair of sneakers. I ushered him in, sat him down, gave him a cup of the very fine brew. His hands shook and he reeked of booze. Did I feel a twinge of guilt over my part in him drinking?

Not really.

He was a priest.

Priests drank.

He said,

"I tried to visit you in hospital, but your brother barred me, said, 'The man is sick, priests he doesn't need.'"

"He's not my brother."

Pat sighed.

"Why is everything about you so complicated?"

He sank into the sofa, let out a breath, asked,

"Can you give me a drink?"

The state of him, I poured a measure into a mug and put it into his shaking hands. He knocked it back, shuddered, closed his eyes, and groaned.

"Don't throw up on my couch."

After a few minutes, he righted himself, asked,

"Another?"

No fucking way.

I said,

"You need to be dried out, you don't want to go into the jigs. I've been there many times, and you are just not the type to weather that."

He reached into his jeans, pulled out the drunkard's roll, i.e., a mess of tangled notes that leak coins every which way. He snarled,

"If it's paying you want?"

I asked,

"What happened to you?"

He leaned back into the sofa, the essence of despair, said,

"I've never been right since Malachy."

Me neither.

Malachy was the priest friend of my bitch mother and the bane of my life. Somehow or other he inveigled me to help him out of his various crises and never once showed an iota of gratitude. Then he got serious cancer, the type that screams,

Don't plan for Christmas.

And he freaked me out by asking me to help him on his way.

I refused but stalled him by saying I'd have to think about it. As other crazy events spiraled round me, he slipped away. He's buried in Rahoon cemetery, and he'd hate that, hate that he wasn't in town.

Pat said,

"He liked you; you know."

He didn't but I let it slide. I asked,

"How are you, um . . ."

Pause.

"Doing priestly stuff in your condition?"

He gave a bitter laugh, said,

"They suspended me."

"On full pay I hope."

He gave me the look, the one that says,

Seriously?

I said,

"You need to be in hospital, to be dried out."

He shook his head.

"And who might I ask will pay for that?"

I said,

"I will."

"When anyone asks me about the Irish character,
I say,
'Look at the trees.'
Maimed,
Stark
and
Misshapen,
But
Ferociously tenacious."

—Edna O'Brien

8

Pat was adamant that he wouldn't go to rehab. I asked,

"Have you had the DTs yet?"

With the defiance of the full-blown alkie, he scoffed,

"You mean do I see pink elephants?"

"You should be so lucky, I'm talking about rabid rats, crawling all over you and the screams you hear are your own."

That got to him,

"Did that happen to you?"

I told the truth, said,

"More times than I'd admit."

He asked,

"How long would I be in rehab?"

I didn't know, he was long along the path, but I lied,

"Tops? A week."

He had the cunning of the seasoned alkie, tried,

"If I agree, will you give me a drink now?"

I gave him what we call the codding drink, more water than booze, but he seemed to buy it. There was so much drink in his system that even a sip brought it up to nigh full throttle.

A banging on the door.

I muttered,

"Better be bloody important."

Opened it to Sheila, who barged past me, fury oozing from her. She was taken aback to see I had company. I said,

"What's bugging you?"

She whirled round, said,

"There's been a third attack."

Shocked, I like a fool said,

"Well, it wasn't me."

Bad, I know.

She stared at Pat, who was dozing. She asked me,

"Are you housing the homeless?"

Pat did look, well, like a street person. He rallied, snarled,

"I'm a priest."

I intervened.

"Father Pat, meet ex-nun Sheila Winston."

Neither spoke so I asked,

"Who was attacked and where, when?"

She gave me the details, and added,

"To make it even more horrific, he laid her on the altar."

Pat, lost completely, asked,

"Who attacked whom?"

"Some psycho is attacking nuns."

He managed to get to his feet and, without asking, helped himself to a drink, offered the bottle to Sheila. She pursed her lips, said,

"It's not even noon yet."

He shrugged.

"You're still a nun."

Sheila gave me the details of the latest attack and I asked,

"In a church?"

Pat intoned,

"You'd be amazed at what happens in churches."

I said,

"God Almighty, no wonder they suspended your arse."

Sheila fixed me with a withering look.

"What progress have you made?"

I was going to lay out the inquiries I'd made but went with,

"None."

She was livid, snarled,

"Spent the money on booze no doubt."

I was very tired of this assembly of weird clergy in my home.

"I need you all to fuck off out of my apartment."

Shocked them both if in different ways. Sheila said,

"No need for the foul language."

Pat whined,

"What about my rehab?"

I did know many folks in the rehab industry, and after a third call, got a result, albeit after promising a donation.

"You need to be ready; they're sending a van and should be here shortly."

He asked,

"Will you come with me?"

I lied,

"They don't allow that."

He was now frightened.

"What will they do to me?"

I tried for bonhomie, not a tone I had much practice with.

"Two days to dry you out, then a few days to get some nourishment into you, and then you're good to go."

Sheila looked highly dubious at this but kept her counsel, perhaps because of the look I shot her.

Pat said,

"Why does nobody get Edge to stop the killings?"

Indeed.

I spoke,

"Apparently, they don't like to get tangled up in matters ecclesiastical."

The rehab I'd managed to get him into was bottom of the barrel. The top places insisted on a patient being dry for a week before. As if an alkie getting a week on the dry would then go for counselling. The donation I'd promised was the overriding factor in his being accepted. After lockdown, all charities and such places like rehab were hurting for donations.

Within the hour, there was a knock on the door, and I opened it to two guys in dark tracksuits, they had the grim faces of serious business.

At first, they thought it was me they were bringing, and God knows, no mystery why they thought that. Sheila took control, took Pat by the shoulder, whispering to him, and within minutes, he was gone.

Sold down the whiskey river.

A silence descended on the apartment until Sheila said,

"I will pray for him."

With bitterness leaking all over my voice, I muttered,

"That is sure to be a massive help."

The Deutschland *sank in December 1875.*
Sixty passengers were drowned.
Among them:
Five Franciscan nuns who had been expelled from Germany
Because of the anticlerical laws.

9

I said to Sheila,

"Surely the Guards have some leads by now?"

She shook her head, said,

"The Mother Superior is good friends with the Guards Superintendent, and he put extra men on the case, but nothing, lots of false leads,
tips, and the sorrow of it is, the public are not outraged, not for a nun
in this time of the Tuam babies' scandal."

In my youth, nuns were revered, more from fear than respect, but
those days were in the wind. I said,

"Sister Maeve, my late friend, gave the nuns a good image, but now?"

She looked heartbroken but I pushed,

"A smart lady like you, you'd have been a good image for them, but
gee, guess what, you legged it. Why did you leave the sinking ship?"

She said simply,

"I lost my faith."

Stark truth.

I had no comment on that and she asked,

"Will you meet with the Mother Superior?"

What?

I asked,

"Why on earth would I do that?"

Sheila looked at me, a plea wide in her eyes.

"Your reputation for finding answers impressed her."

I said,

"Now, Sister, that is a barefaced lie."

Sheila considered, then,

"She's really desperate."

"I'm the last resort, that it?"

I met with the Mother Superior on a cold December morning, you could see your breath in the air. I was wrapped in Item 1834, my all-weather Guard coat. I'm not sure what I expected the Mother Superior to be, but I was met by a warm middle-aged woman in a heavy habit, the large crucifix hanging down looked like it weighed a ton. She saw me inspect it, said,

"We all have our burdens."

No argument there.

She motioned to me to sit on a single hard chair before a large desk. She took her seat, interlocked her fingers, asked,

"Might I call you Jack?"

I nodded and she gave a short tight smile.

I said,

"You're not what I was expecting."

She laughed.

"And what would that be?"

Tell the truth, shame the devil. I said,

"A severe Mother Superior, a lot older than you."

That amused her.

"The sisters here might agree with the severity part."

She had green eyes that held a mix of strength and amusement; if I wasn't careful, I might like her. I said,

"Three of your nuns have been attacked and, in all honesty, I don't know how to help."

"Jack, you have a reputation for finding answers where the situation seems impossible, and in truth, we don't know what to do."

I suggested,

"Travel in pairs."

She sighed, said,

"Would that we could but our sisters are stretched to breaking point with our work in and for the community."

I put my hand in my jacket, produced two small canisters, laid them softly on the table. She stared at them.

"Not holy water, I'd say."

"Pepper spray."

When she seemed puzzled, I said,

"Shoot it into the attacker's eyes and he'll not only be blinded but in excruciating pain."

She was shocked, took a moment, then,

"My sisters couldn't possibly carry such a lethal thing."

She studied me, said,

"He rang me."

I was stunned, gasped,

"The attacker?"

She nodded and I prodded,

"It could be any lunatic."

"It was him."

So, you'd have to ask, and I did,

"How on earth can you be sure?"

She was silent, weighing up her answer, then,

"I know pure evil when I encounter it."

My mind was in overdrive.

"We'll put a trace on your phone."

Her head shook.

"You'll do no such thing, we're a convent not some covert operation."

I wanted to shake her, asked,

"What about I shadow your nuns as they go about their business?"

No way.

She said,

"That wouldn't do at all, I can't allow a man to follow my sisters around."

This was infuriating.

"There is already a very vicious predator following them."

I tried another tack and asked,

"On the phone, did he have an accent, young or old?"

She looked ashamed.

"He asked me to pick a number."

"Pick a number, I don't get it."

Head down, she said,

"I don't know what I was thinking but I blurted six without even thinking."

I got it.

She raised her head, and I could see she'd forced herself not to weep, too much steel.

"What have I done?"

"He was toying with you. It's a game, a sick one."

She asked the question on both our minds.

"Does he mean he will attack three more nuns?"

Yup.

I said,

"Who can guess what weird thoughts he had."

In my mind, but thank God I didn't voice it, was,

What if you'd said fifteen?

I then said,

"There's talk of an outfit called Edge who administer justice."

She scoffed, went,

"That's an urban legend."

There was little more I could add, she pretty much shot down any suggestions I made. I said,

"I'll head off then."

She stood up, looked like she might embrace me.

God in heaven.

A hug from a nun.

She reached in her habit, took out a thin silver chain with a medal on it. I nearly said,

"Whoa, hold the thought, Sister, I'm all done with relics."

But managed to keep my mouth shut.

She put it round my neck.

"This is Saint Faustina, the miracle worker for healing."

I tucked it inside my shirt, wanted to say,

"Gee, I feel better already."

I said,

"Thank you."

She assessed me, said in a quiet tone,

"I know you don't believe in it, but you wear it and I'll do the belief."

Fair enough.

She said,

"Our sister, Sheila, said you might be difficult, but I think you're just a little lost."

Amen.

Outside I was accosted by a wino who asked for help. I gave him Saint Faustina.

THE
    BURNING
            OF
        THE WINOS

10

Scott Williams was sixteen years old and vicious for every one of those years. Cruelty was his gig. He was a good-looking kid, could have passed for a minor Brad Pitt. His cruelty was matched by his superciliousness.

Early in his teens, he had learned to hide his true nature. He had been caught trapping a cat and barely managed to escape serious repercussions. If he hadn't been caught, he would have set the animal on fire.

His neighborhood was almost completely free of felines due to his earlier efforts. Helping with his narrow escape was money.

Shitloads of it.

An only child, his mother adored him, and both she and her husband were fuck-the-world rich.

The cat woman whose pet had been trapped got a fat check for her silence and she used it to buy a dog. She named the dog Rich.

Scott had a buddy, a boy named Tony Wren, from a middle-class background, fourteen years of age and, according to his teachers, the boy was slow. Cancel culture had recently made an issue of the r-word.

Tony had come across Scott when Scott had just trapped one of his early cats. Scott had the animal in a net when Tony came upon them; he asked,

"Whatcha doing?"

Scott looked at the boy. He knew him from school and had heard he was a nutjob.

Instinct played a large part in what ensued.

Scott produced a gold lighter and a can of lighter fluid, looked at Tony, and asked,

"Wanna play?"

No one had ever asked Tony to play. Scott was smiling at him, and it made Tony feel like a player. He said,

"You betcha."

Scott handed him the lighter, said,

"You gotta be fast. I'm going to release the little bastard, douse him, and you have to get him before he bolts, got it?"

The cat was released, and Tony missed him, fumbled the lighter. He expected wrath from Scott, who said,

"No biggie, I have more."

And he did.

On the third attempt, Tony got it right and lit up the poor animal; the screeches from the creature delighted Scott.

Tony not so much.

But he faked it, said,

"Awesome."

Folie à deux, the shrinks call it, when two psychos hook up, like the Hillside Stranglers. Usually in this lethal pairing, one is the alpha male. The other is like a brainwashed follower but fully cognizant of their deeds.

Over the following weeks, they embarked on a series of events.

Bullying of younger children.

More animals.

Burglaries.

And building up a supply of booze pinched from Scott's father's well-stocked cabinet. Scott had a shed at the bottom of their lavish garden, gift from Daddy, and they turned it into their den of iniquity. Books lined one wall, all detailing Columbine and other school shootings.

They didn't have access to guns but lived in sick hope.

Scott had secured the basement tapes in which the Columbine killers sneered.

Snarled.

Planned.

Murder and mayhem.

They watched it a hundred times.

A Saturday afternoon, they were drinking Southern Comfort, shooting the breeze. Tony, always anxious to impress Scott, said,

"Shall we get some cats?"

Scott, built-in sneer in place, said,

"It's getting a little old, time to move up."

Tony didn't know what that meant, asked,

"How'd you mean?"

Scott smiled.

"People."

That scared Tony but a part of him thrilled to it. He asked,

"Who do we burn?"

Scott stared at him, thought,

Fucking loser.

Said,

"I hate winos."

Scott didn't share that he had once tried to piss on a homeless person who was far from a victim and got his arse seriously kicked.

That evening, they prowled Eyre Square, lots of potential targets but in groups. Scott imagined dousing the lot of them and having a sensational inferno, contented himself with,

"Later."

They found a woman slumped in a doorway, near Merchants Road, and there was little foot traffic. Scott said,

"Let's heat her up."

But Tony had only enough petrol to douse her legs and Scott snarled,

"You are a fucking idiot."

Tony felt the lash as if he'd been whipped. He asked,

"Shall we just leave her?"

Scott rolled his eyes, produced a box of matches, struck one.

"Time to burn, bitch."

Raftery had saved my life and yet I knew fuck all about him.

We were having a quiet pint in Garavan's, and I asked,

"Who are you really?"

He said,

"Not to give you a short answer but I'm rich."

I drained half my pint, it was one of the rich, creamy ones, why we drink it. I asked,

"What the hell does that mean?"

He signaled for a fresh round, turned to me.

"Jack, being rich means never having to explain."

"That is horseshit. You know just about everything about me, so unless you share some stuff, I'm out of here."

He considered this, then,

"I'm half-Irish on my mother's side, the very rich side. I worked as an accountant after the Marines, then my mum died and left me shed loads of property. Now I run a podcast."

What?

He explained that to me and said it was titled:

Galway Confidential.

I asked,

"And what, people listen to you?"

He gave a large smile.

"Thirty thousand and change."

I was puzzled, pushed,

"But there are other podcasts out there, right?"

His smile faltered. He said,

"A few."

I was no nearer comprehension.

"So why listen to you?"

He thought about it, then said,

"Crime, I report on that."

A thought hit me.

"Any money in it?"

He gave a satisfied smile, said,

"We have a steady stream of revenue, it spiked when you were the topic."

I didn't know if this was a good thing.

"So, people cared?"

He shrugged.

"They were interested but that's a long way from actual caring."

Asked and bluntly answered.

He asked me how the hunt for the nun assailant was progressing.

I said,

"Going nowhere, there hasn't been an attack for a few weeks so maybe he's gone away."

He said,

"You don't believe that."

True.

A new strain of the virus was sweeping the world, named Omicron. Almost immediately scare stories abounded.

It spread faster than Delta, more virulent, immune to the vaccines.

Talk of returning to the severe restrictions were fast circulating.

Thirty hurricanes swept through the southern states of America, Kentucky was the worst hit. Sky News was showing scenes of utter devastation.

Raftery said to me,

"See, you legalize abortion and God unleashes plagues upon the world."

I gave him a long look, said,

"Didn't have you down as a religious fanatic."

He gave a sad laugh, said,

"Oh, Jack, this isn't about religion, this is about retribution."

I had no answer to that. Is there one?

Confidence in a man
Is
Viewed with admiration.
Confidence in a woman
Is
Viewed with suspicion.

11

Scott was furious that their burning of the wino appeared to have gone unnoticed, not a single word in the paper. Tony said,

"Maybe it's better if we keep a low profile."

Scott rounded on him, snarled,

"The fuck does you know, we are going to be famous."

Tony thought jail was the more likely outcome, but he kept that to himself. Best to let Scott's rage burn out, so to speak.

He said,

"What about we burn two together?"

Scott liked it, a lot.

"We're going to need a bigger can."

Across from the docks was a sheltered overhang and a man and woman had claimed it as their spot. The boys watched them for a few nights, and usually round midnight they settled down under a canopy of cardboard on the tarmac. Scott said,

"That's our folk."

They had two Coke bottles full of petrol and a large box of kitchen matches. They dressed in dark clothes, smoked a ton of weed washed down with Jack Daniels. Adrenaline had them high as kites.

They approached the couple slowly. The woman appeared to be singing

"Peggy Gordon."

And the man was humming along. Scott took the top off his bottle, splashed it over them both, nodded to Tony, saying,

"Things go better with Coke."

The fire took hold instantly and the couple were engulfed. Tony muttered,

"Holy shit."

Scott was a bit shocked at the ferocity of the flames and grabbed Tony's arm, shouted,

"We need to get the fuck out of here."

Tony seemed to be stricken in place, the screams of the couple transfixed him. Scott slapped him hard in the face.

"Get it together, what did you expect?"

Tony had no answer, in truth he thought the fire would singe rather than blaze. He said,

"I feel sick."

Scott laughed.

"Not as sick as those two."

Scott finally dragged him away, with Tony casting backward glances, as if the couple might yet follow them.

Back at Scott's shed, they drank large tumblers of Southern Comfort, Tony could swear he tasted ash in his. Scott was flying, wild excitement coursing through him. He pulled a large whiteboard down along the wall, used a marker to scribble

1.

2.

3.

His eyes were shining with madness, euphoria run riot. He said,

"I want to see thirty on that board, you hear me? Thirty of the useless fucks on fire."

Tony stumbled out of the shed and threw up his guts.

12

Over the years, I've been always friendly with

Drinking schools,

Unemployed,

Winos.

As I full realize, I am but a Jameson away from joining them and they recognize a fellow pilgrim on the grim road. Geary, a man who'd survived nigh ten years on the street, had witnessed near most of the evil the world has to offer, and once said to me,

"We can somehow stomach the nasty shite they do to us, but the very worst is indifference, to be invisible."

He had got a message to me that he needed to see me as soon as possible. We didn't meet in a pub, he wouldn't be allowed in. We met on his territory, Eyre Square, at the bottom end where a large tree provides a meager shelter. His age was impossible to gauge as his face was so weather-beaten. He had two coats and a battered baseball cap. His pants were Gore-Tex, a gift from me own self. His shoes had once been impressive brogues but were now very worn. He had kind blue eyes, that type that the world had dimmed but failed to extinguish.

He gave me a lopsided grin.

"You've been AWOL for years, brother."

"In a coma."

He gave a nervous laugh. He said,

"Like most of this city."

We sat on the small wall there and he produced a bottle.

"I'd offer you a swig, but unless you're accustomed to it, it would put you back in your coma."

He drank deep, gave a small shudder, gasped,

Phew-oh.

I asked,

"Are you on the housing list?"

He shrugged.

"I'm not a priority."

He reached in his coat, produced a very tattered wallet with a faded Celtic cross on the front, reached into it, and took out a band of crumpled notes; he saw me glance at the wallet, said,

"My ex-wife gave me that, it's the only remnant of our marriage. The house, kids, her own self, just blown on the wind of my drinking."

He thought about that for a while, then,

"I knew I had to either leave or stop drinking when I realized that the smiles on my children's faces evaporated when I came home."

He paused, swallowed hard, continued,

"I chose the booze and here I am."

He looked at me, said,

"Don't you dare pity me, Jack."

I didn't.

I said,

"I'm not renowned for smart moves my own self."

And he laughed.

"Why we love you, Jack."

He offered me the tangle of notes, said,

"There's more there than it looks, you learn on the street to make a lot look less."

I asked,

"Why are you offering me money?"

He was quiet for a time, then,

"Someone is burning our people."

He told of three winos who had been attacked, said,

"And there'll be more. One of the victims heard the assailants laughing, so they are getting off on it, means there will be more."

I was supposed to be hunting the nun perpetrator and could ill afford to split my time. I tried,

"The Guards?"

He gave a bitter laugh.

"Yeah right, some winos getting burnt, that's going to be really important to them."

I looked at the money, asked,

"Are you hiring me?"

He nodded.

I handed the money back to him.

"I'll try but I can't promise anything."

He gave me a long look, said,

"Jack, you have solved cases that no one else would even attempt."

I told the truth.

"Cases got solved around me, very rarely did I actually find the solution."

He put his hand in his coat again, took out the fixings of a smoke, rolled one expertly, handed it to me, then rolled another. He took out a box of those old-time Swan matches, fired us up. The first inhale had me coughing hard and I managed,

Phew-oh.

He laughed.

"Like life on the road, harsh is what we do."

I asked,

"Where are the places that your people might use to get away from people?"

"There are no such refuges, but I can give you the name of a few streets that are less exposed than others."

I made a note of them, and he asked,

"Will you work alone or have help?"

I thought of Raftery.

"Maybe, but I prefer to work alone."

He guessed,

"Lone wolf, eh?"

"No."

I said,

"People get hurt around me."

He took another deep swig of his bottle and almost unconsciously handed it to me. I took it, took a breath, and chugged. God Almighty, it kicked like a bull, my eyes watered, and my heart did a reel and a jig. I didn't ask what it was, some things you truly are better off not knowing.

He gave me a studied look, then,

"See, Jack, you're a class act. I gave you the bottle after I'd drank from it and you . . ."

Pause.

"Didn't wipe the rim."

Truth to tell, it had crossed my mind, but some granite etiquette still lingered there. He spoke,

"All kinds of folk pass through here and the ones I despise are the ones who try to make me their good deed."

He stood up, said,

"I must go, rustle up some grub. I try to eat every day if the Good Lord wills it. I rarely have an appetite, my thirst, alas, knows no bounds. It has a demonic grip, that drink, but times are, it kicks in and I feel like a kind of fleeting peace. I must blot out all thoughts of my abandoned family, but those brief moments when the booze sings in my blood, that's what I live for."

He put out his hand, said,

"Not supposed to touch with the Covid rules but I'll always shake your hand, Jack, no virus is stopping that."

I took his hand, and his grip was surprisingly strong. I was moved in ways I'd near forgotten.

"I'll do my best for you and your people."

He gave a short smile, said,

"You always have."

I got to the top of the square and a very respectable-looking man approached. He looked vaguely familiar. He greeted,

"Remember me? You gave me the Saint Faustina medal, the saint of healing. Well, I've been sober ever since, not a drop."

I had nothing, but tried,

"Miraculous."

He looked like he might hug me but went with,

"I owe you man."

I added,

"And Faustina."

"Funeral of a friend"

Ashen
Was
The way I felt
When shunned again
By people
I had
Justi-fied
Didn't all
That much
Really
Warrant grief.

       —Raftery, 2001

13

That very night, Geary was burned to death.

I was with Owen Daglish, one of the very few Guards willing to talk to me. To be even seen with me could have an adverse effect on their careers. We were in Hardiman's hotel, previously.

The Mercyk.

The Great Southern.

And now in its new incantation, looking pretty much like its previous forms. We were there as it was unlikely we'd meet anyone we knew.

I was so angry I could spit. I snarled at Owen,

"What do you mean the Guards have no clue as to who burned my friend to death?"

Owen was a big man, Guinness and hurling had made him formidable and his temper was as short as my own.

"Watch the tone, Jack."

We were drinking coffee and the caffeine was fueling my rage. I said,

"Surely the number of homeless deaths is suspicious to even the Guards?"

He said in a quiet tone,

"We have a special unit on it."

I knew all about special units, meant you couldn't quiz them or even know who was involved. A waitress was passing, and I asked her for a large Jameson, asked Owen if he wanted one, he did.

I said to Owen,

"Maybe you could set up another unit to find the psycho who is attacking nuns."

He took a deep breath.

"You're skirting very close to the edge here, Jack. I could be in deep shite for just being seen with you so how about you lower the sarcasm. I'm not the enemy."

The drinks arrived. We didn't have anything to toast so drank in fuming silence for a bit, then Owen said,

"There is a kid named Scott Williams who has been shouting his mouth off about ridding the city of winos."

"Who is he?"

Owen took out a notebook.

"He's a dumb fuck who has been in minor skirmishes with the law, but burning people, that would be a huge step up for him."

I had to think about this. Owen added,

"Jack, leave this to the Guards. If he's involved, then you can be sure we'll nail him."

I asked,

"There's two of them. Who does he hang with?"

He shook his head.

"You have to back off this, Jack."

I finished my drink, said,

"Thanks for the help."

He looked at me.

"Thing with you, Jack, it's hard to know if you're being sarcastic."

I gave him my best smile.

"If you're in doubt, you can be sure it's sarcasm."

Who buries the lost? The
Marginalized,
Homeless,
The castaways.

14

I went to the inquest on Geary, and the coroner recorded a verdict of misadventure. After asking three different officials, I was directed to a man who was riffling through a sheaf of papers. He had glasses perched on his nose and looked at me over them.

"Was there something?"

His tone suggested there was nothing I had to offer. I asked,

"Are you the guy who's responsible for the unclaimed deceased?"

He seemed already short of patience, snapped,

"It is one of my functions."

He had the kind of face that you know has never really been walloped properly but I could amend that.

"I want to pay for the burial of Mr. Geary."

He rolled his eyes and, before he thought about it, asked,

"Why?"

I could give him a hundred reasons but settled for,

"None of your business."

He considered this, then leafed through his papers, took one out, and handed it to me, said,

"Give this to the undertaker."

I stood for the briefest of moments, then,

"Thank you for the tremendous help, you are a credit to whatever job it is you have."

He thought about a response but decided against it.

"You're welcome."

※

The day we buried Geary, the heavens opened, lashed down with rain. Around ten homeless people were present, and the priest gave the usual dirge about man being full of woe. I wanted to add,

"And homeless."

We weren't going to be allowed to have a wake or reception in a hotel when they saw the state of the mourners. I had brought along a crate of booze and a box of sandwiches; after the burial, we huddled under a tree and toasted Geary. The gravediggers joined us and one of them asked,

"Who paid for this shindig?"

"I did."

He looked round at the huddled people, said,

"You need your head examined."

The rain eased and as the Jameson took hold a woman sang,

"She moves through the fair."

And for some odd reason, it seemed to fit.

Raftery said to me,

"You paid for the funeral?"

We were in Garavan's; after a few bright, brittle days of sunshine, we were now having heavy, thundery showers, the type that seem personal and are determined to drench you.

"He was a friend."

Raftery finished his pint, signaled for another round. The rain gave serious motivation to not moving. I liked to watch the pouring of a pint, it's such a delicate art; near fill the glass, let it sit, and then add that creamy head, smooth it off with a plain stick.

Art.

"I was thinking of doing a podcast on you."

I said in a low voice,

"Don't."

Which shut down that thread.

I said,

"I could do with your help, though."

I told him of the guy who might be one of the arsonists, and said,

"You could ask your audience if they knew anybody fitting the vague description we have and say he's won a prize or some such bullshit."

I thought it hadn't a hope in hell of working.

I was wrong.

Confidential

   Is regarded

   In Ireland

   As

   Something to hide.

15

New measures had the pubs closing at eight. Totally useless as that was the time people headed to the pubs. The hospitals were fighting for their very survival as the new strain, Omicron, took hold. Despair was the prevalent mood of the country.

Christmas came, a very muted affair. I kept my head down, drank quietly, and tried not to think of all the people I had lost. New Year came in with a whimper and nothing on the horizon inspired any joy.

The Serbian tennis ace Djokovic was not allowed into Australia for the Tennis Open as he was not vaccinated; he claimed special dispensation but couldn't produce the documentation to prove it.

I was reading about the guilty verdict on Ghislaine Maxwell when my doorbell went. I opened it to Father Pat, did a quick calculation in my head, and yeah, figured he had lasted the rehab course. I said,

"Come in."

He looked fit and healthy, dressed in casual jeans and trainers.

"Sit down. Can I get you something to, um . . . maybe coffee or . . . ?"

He gave a broad smile, said,

"No need to be careful about mentioning Jameson, I'm in a whole different space now, but a coffee would be good."

Got that squared away and said,

"So, the treatment worked."

Another big smile.

"I won't lie to you, Jack, it was harsh in the beginning, but after a few weeks, I accepted the fact I'm an alcoholic."

Do you congratulate someone for this or go,

Uh-huh.

I went with that.

He said,

"If you ever feel the need to change your own life path, Jack, I'm here for you."

Fuck.

I was saved from answering by a knock on the door, opened it to Sheila Winston and, I shit you not, she was carrying a bottle of Jameson. She said,

"Happy New Year."

Then she saw Pat, whose eyes were glued to the bottle of hooch. I waved her in.

"Pat, you met Sheila Winston, an ex-nun. I don't where you guys stand on the whole deserting ship thing, but she seems harmless."

Pat stood up; as handshakes were no longer used, he tried that awkward elbow greeting, it just looks wrong. I asked,

"So why are you bringing me gifts?"

She placed the bottle on the coffee table, about a millimeter from Pat.

"Jack, I don't know how you did it but there have been no further attacks."

I didn't want to spoil her moment but knew that another attack would surely come.

Pat picked up the bottle and cracked the seal, sniffed deep, said,

"Don't fret, Jack, I'm only smelling it. Not a chance of me actually drinking it."

I said,

"Seems like tempting fate."

He gave a hollow laugh.

"But let me pour you guys a tipple, no reason for ye to go without."

In unison, we both near screamed,

"No."

A strange expression crossed his face. He said,

"Well, shame to waste it."

And—

Drank.

There was a silence in the room, as if someone had just died, and in a fashion, someone just did.

Pat put the cap back on the bottle.

"See, I don't need any more. I can take it or leave it."

I moved and swiped the bottle off the table, said,

"You ejit, you'll be licking it off the floor before the day is done."

Sheila tried to intervene.

"That's a little harsh, Jack."

I rounded on her, snarled,

"Harsh? I'll tell you what's harsh, the complete and utter devastation that sip will wreak on his life."

Pat laughed nervously, said,

"You're one to talk, you're still around despite worse drinking than I did."

I took a deep breath.

"I was raised rough, lived rough, and sometimes I know when to back off the booze; if you live to be fifty, which I doubt, you'll never survive the mental disintegration coming down the pike."

He stood up.

"Well, I better be going. I have to meet the Bishop to see if I'm to be reassigned to a parish."

I said,

"Eat a lot of mints and try not to share your thoughts on alcohol."

He said goodbye to Sheila and to me.

"You'll see, Jack, I'll be fine."

I said,

"You'll be a lot of things but fine isn't going to be one of them."

※

After Pat had left, still defiant, and defiance is the outstanding characteristic of the alcoholic, Sheila said,

"Maybe he'll be all right."

"He won't."

She seemed lost for a way back into the conversation, terse as it was.

"Mother Superior was impressed by you."

I gave her the long look—*you're kidding, right?*

And I asked,

"What impressed her?"

Sheila didn't have to flounder, came right back with,

"Your honesty."

That was a first. I've been called most things and few of them in the virtue column, so I gave a tight smile, tried,

"I liked her, too, she's feisty."

Sheila gave a warm smile.

"You're welcome in the convent anytime."

"You have to impress upon the nuns to walk in pairs, this guy is not finished."

She prepared to leave, touched my arm.

"You be careful, Jack."

I said,

"I will."

Then added,

"Honest."

16

Sister Aloysius liked the quiet shrine beside St. Patrick's church. It was well back from the road and yet within a prayer of the parish priest's house. Mother Superior would be angry she was on her own but how long could one decade of the rosary take?

Almost out of nowhere, a man appeared. He was dressed in black and stood about five yards from her. He was carrying a backpack, and she estimated his age at about thirty. He was of average height, regular features. He gave her a warm smile, asked,

"Is it safe for a nun to be out alone these days?"

And something in his tone chilled her. She said,

"My friend is in the church and will be out any moment."

He let out a long sigh.

"A lying nun, that's not good."

His body was relaxed, as if he had all the time in the world. She moved to get past him, and he said,

"Ah, you can't leave without knowing what's in the bag."

He reached in the rucksack, took out a hammer.

"One whack for the lie and maybe a second whack just for the hell of it."

She made a rush to his right, but he almost lazily punched her in the face, asked,

"What's your hurry?"

Sheila was inconsolable. I was with her in the corridor of the hospital as the doctors fought to save the life of Sister Aloysius. She was banging her head against the wall, muttering,

"You were right, Jack, why didn't I listen?"

I had no answer for that. A tall man approached, showed a warrant card, said,

"Detective Walsh. Might I have a few words with you, Mr. Taylor?"

We moved to a secluded area of the corridor, and he said,

"I've been assigned to the case."

I wanted to snap,

About fucking time.

But bit down, waited.

He said,

"Can you tell me what you know about the other attacks?"

I gave him all I had, which was pityingly little. He made a few notes, then asked,

"How come the nuns came to you for help? I mean no offense, but what did they think you could accomplish?"

There was an edge to his tone now but that was okay.

I can do edge.

"They got tired of asking you lot for help."

Before he could respond, I added,

"Plus, I'm cheap."

Raftery said,

"The podcast threw up a few names of likely suspects, but they came to nothing."

For a dizzying few moments I didn't know which case he was referring to.

The arsonists?

The nun predator?

The world was spinning out of the slim circles remaining.

One hundred thousand Russian troops were assembled at the border of Ukraine. In the US, Trump's troops seemed to be reignited, and Joe Biden was proving to be a lame duck.

The Omicron variant of the virus appeared to have peaked in Ireland and we waited anxiously for hospital admissions to fall. It was like a collective holding of breath.

Parties at 10 Downing Street threatened to oust Boris Johnson, even hard-core Tories were aghast at him.

On the 18th of January, at 11:00 A.M., the country held a moment's silence for the murdered twenty-three-year-old teacher Ashling Murphy. She had been out jogging along the canal, a route well-worn by many walkers, when she was attacked by a man. She had fought ferociously and left him with injuries. The chief suspect was now in hospital, with the Guards waiting to interview him.

Ten thousand people turned up for a vigil. It was one of those moments when the whole country united in its grief. The stretch of ground Aisling had been on was known as Fiona Pinder Walk in memory of a young pregnant woman who had disappeared from that very spot.

The heated debate on the violence of men against women was everywhere.

"Confidential

Means when translated

To Irish

The exaggeration of a secret."

—Overheard in Ireland

on January 26, 2021

17

The Russians have told us they will be performing exercises off our southern coast! Cork fishermen told them,

"That's what you think."

Never fuck with a Cork fisherman!

The country is gripped by the story of three men in a post office in Carlow. The postmistress refused to pay pension money to the man in the middle as he was, she said,

"Looking decidedly unwell."

He was in fact dead.

Two men had walked the dead man from across the town, with his sweater pulled up to his face, and wearing a face mask (so following the health regulations).

When the payout of his pension was refused, the two men leaned him against the wall and left.

The men later claimed that the man had just died at the counter.

I was walking along the Salthill promenade when I literally keeled over. No drink taken. Just out of nowhere, flat on my face.

And lost another two months of my life.

I woke up in hospital again, muttering,

"Fucking Groundhog Day."

A doctor came in.

"How are we?"

We!

I spoke,

"I've done this gig before."

He had my chart in his hands, said,

"Indeed, we have, but this time it was months, not years, so progress is being made."

He went on to tell me that a slight lesion on my brain, not cancerous, he hastened to add, had caused the fall. They had operated and, in his words, got it all. I put up my hand, asked,

"But how am I now?"

"You are good to go. We need some sessions of physical therapy but considering the life you have led, you are some sort of medical anomaly."

I nearly laughed.

"Last time round, they said I was a miracle. Have I been demoted?"

He nearly allowed himself a smile, said,

"Miracles are overrated, and we use the term sparingly."

"What did I miss?"

He looked confused, tried,

"In life?"

I said carefully,

"The world, Covid, Omicron, Brexit?"

He looked crestfallen, then,

"Russia invaded Ukraine."

Showstopper.

He gave me a brief overview of the Ukraine situation; already, three million people had fled their homeland. Europe was accepting refugees daily. Ireland had already welcomed nigh on twenty thousand people, they arrived exhausted after days of arduous travel across Europe, their menfolk left behind to try and fight the Russians. We were sending lorry loads of aid, especially medical aid, to Ukraine.

The narrative was so grim, tragic, and heartbreaking that I almost wished I was still unconscious.

I tried to remember what I had been doing before my latest coma. Slowly, it came back, the attacks on the homeless people, the psycho attacking nuns, and I felt a wave of exhaustion.

As the doctor prepared to leave, he said,

"You need a radical change of lifestyle; you can't continue as you've been."

I wanted to shout,

"What I need is a large Jay, and a cigarette wouldn't hurt either."

He left and I lay there, the swirls of a broken world all around me. A nurse breezed in, greeted,

"You're back with us yet again, Jack."

And following behind her came Raftery. He didn't seem too fazed to see me awake, but then he was a guy who kept quiet on most all he felt or didn't feel.

He had a flask and the nurse said,

"I'm very sorry, Mr. Raftery, but we are under strict orders to inspect any beverage you produce."

He handed her the flask, said,

"It's finest Colombian roast and you are welcome to a shot of it."

She took the top off, sniffed, looked dubious, but finally put the top back, said,

"That's fine."

She left and Raftery unscrewed the top of the flask, used the metal top/cup and poured a half measure, looked round him, pulled out a half bottle of Jay, laced the coffee, handed it to me.

I had a moment of indecision, but then,

Fuckit!

It hit my stomach like a warm kick. I asked what the world was doing about Ukraine.

He gave me a long, detailed account of what NATO and the UN were saying and in summary said,

"So, nothing."

He told of how Zelensky, the Ukrainian president, gave daily briefings of the atrocities against children and civilians, and the incessant bombardment of the cities. He refused to take refuge in the West, stayed by his people.

We raised a silent toast to him and his country.

※

Russian influencers and models
On learning that Chanel would no longer do business
With Russia
Cut up their Chanel merchandise.

※

It was time to do something about the attacks on the homeless. I knew that the vulnerable places were where you found few people.

No witnesses.

I got a thermal sleeping bag, battered it to get that worn look, got thermal underwear, watch cap, gloves, and my hurly. A flask for my Jay-laden coffee and I was ready to roll. As I surveyed my provisions, there was a knock at the door. Opened it to Sheila Winston, who declared,

"They released you."

She looked great, her face healthy and windblown, as if she had done the Galway walk. You start at The Claddagh, go along by the coast road until you reach Grattan Road, passing the Famine Memorial, made possible by the late Mark Kennedy, a memorial to Celia Griffin, a six-year-old child who died of hunger during the Famine. The names of the ships trying to get the people to America were inscribed on the stone and to read them aloud was like a prayer of the past.

You reached Salthill and walked at a brisk pace along the prom, to Blackrock and the iconic diving towers. There is a stone wall there and the tradition is to kick it, walk completed. Of course, you must come back but that is a whole different story.

I asked her in, offered refreshments as she stared at my supplies. She asked,

"Are you going camping?"

Made me smile.

"After a fashion."

I told her what I was planning, and she was instantly furious, accused.

"Are you stone mad?"

Hmm?

"My sanity has always been open to debate, but somebody has to do something."

"You need to rest up, this plan is crazy."

We tossed that back and forth and finally she left in disgust.

The first night on the street, I set up my vigil off Merchant's Road, around eleven at night. Got the sleeping bag spread out and tentatively pulled it up around me. I couldn't settle on a position, to lie down or sit up? What I wanted was to have easy access to the hurly, and wasted a good half hour deciding on where I should lay it.

Not many people were around and one guy passing sneered,

"Get a fucking job."

Another threw some coppers at me, and I had to restrain myself from clocking him with the hurly. A hen party came screaming along, gathered round me, and offered me slugs of their champagne bottles. One of them leaned in and blew a kiss, said,

"Wrap up warm, darlin'."

That kind of hit my heart, and I swear, I was sorry when they moved on. I took some sips from my flask and let the heat spread in my gut. I was half dozing when I became aware of somebody standing over me. I sat up fast, my hand on the hurly. It was a man in a thick overcoat. He whispered,

"I'll give you twenty euro for a blow job."

Jesus wept.

I stood up, waved the hurly, said,

"Take a hike."

He did.

By five in the morning, I was stiff with the cold and gathered my gear, headed for home. First thing I did was take a shower, didn't shave as I needed the rugged look. My phone rang, it was Sheila. I told her I was home, and nothing had occurred.

"Well, you hardly expected to find the culprit on the first outing."

I said,

"I did get offered twenty euro for a sexual act."

She hung up on me.

My body was aching from the night, and I crawled into bed, and was asleep almost instantly. I dreamed, phew-oh, did I dream!

Of—

Hen parties.

Hurlies.

Ukraine.

Doctors.

The usual fragmented shape of dreams juggled all those elements in a kaleidoscope of anxiety so that I woke eight hours later, the bed drenched in sweat. Told myself,

"You don't need to keep vigil tonight."

Did that fly?

Did it fuck?

18

I cooked myself a steak, medium rare, and lots of spuds. I'd need the fuel for another night on the tiles. I had cans of Guinness in the fridge but couldn't quite bring myself to drink the black from a tin.

It's kind of like a heresy.

I had bought them in a fit of indecision on one of those days I figured I'd give up Jameson.

Right!

I was halfway through the meal and watching Sky News. The onslaught in Ukraine was unrelenting. A train station packed with a thousand civilians, children and women, was hit by two cluster bombs and, shockingly, the shell of one of the bombs had inscribed on it,

"For the children."

As the Russians retreated toward the east, they raped and pillaged like utter psychos. I wanted to turn off the news, turn off my mind, but felt the very least I could do was bear witness. I pushed my dinner aside.

The doorbell chimed and I opened it to Raftery. He was carrying two bags of shopping. He said,

"Beware of geeks bearing gear."

He was dressed in his country-squire gig, tweed jacket and, yes, a cravat, heavy green cords, brogues, and, of course, a tweed cap. I said,

"Brideshead Revisited."

He had brought a pile of food, enough for a small siege. I expressed my thanks and slight puzzlement.

"You don't really do gratitude, Jack."

Bit nasty, I thought, but went with,

"Lemme give you some money. I have plenty as I haven't spent anything for two years, more even."

He waved it away, said,

"This amount of shopping has doubled in price within the last week. Fuel, oil power, everything is up by at least twenty-five percent."

Ukraine.

I poured him a Jay and he toasted me, with,

"Here's to consciousness."

Then he surveyed the sleeping bag and paraphernalia.

"A camping trip?"

I gave him the short version of my mission, said,

"I'm hunting."

He considered this, looked at the hurly.

"Will the hurly be outside the bag, or how do you intend to play that hand?"

I wasn't entirely sure but tried,

"I'm going to make it up as I go along."

He shook his head, said,

"It's a really bad idea."

I could have said how bad ideas were the ones I was most familiar with but instead began to put the groceries in the cupboard and said,

"I do appreciate this."

He finished his drink.

"I'll come with you."

Aw fuck.

I said,

"No, you'd only be in the way."

We tossed this back and forth and finally he gave in. As he prepared to leave, he asked,

"If the perpetrator does show up, what are you intending to do? Beat him senseless?"

I acted as if I was weighing this, then went,

"Great idea."

As he prepared to leave, he said,

"It's my birthday today."

Took me by surprise and I had to refrain from uttering,

"Like I could give a shit."

But said,

"Happy birthday."

He said,

"Back in my Marine days, Quinlan, my treacherous buddy, gave me a bottle of pure vodka on my birthday."

I'd no idea where this was headed.

"Uh-huh."

He said,

"It was the last time anyone gave me a birthday present."

He waited but I had nothing, like zero, to give to this story so he continued,

"I drank gallons of vodka and never once had a hangover."

Now that, that impressed me. Hangovers are the bane of my besotted life. He said,

"Trick was, never quite stop, so the hangover is hovering, but you wallop it with more vodka."

Okay.

Enough.

I asked,

"Are you angling for a gift, is that the point of this whole saga?"

He smiled, said,

"Exactly."

Fuck me.

I spread out my hands, said,

"What do you want?"

He pointed at my night gear, said,

"I'd like a hurly."

"That one you're looking at, it's old. I'll get you a new one, fresh from the ash."

He shook his head, declared,

"I want that one. It's lived in, so to speak."

I wanted to beat him with it.

"I give you the hurly, you figure I won't be sleeping rough tonight?"

He laughed, said,

"As if I'd be so devious."

"Okay, take it, and I'll rely on the sawn-off."

Shocked him.

"You're kidding, aren't you?"

I gave him my best smile, all false bonhomie, said,

"I never joke about weapons."

I spoke,

"Three times I've asked you who the hell you are."

He answered,

"I'm half-American, half-Irish, I was a Marine, I had a friend, Quinlan, who shafted me. I work now as an accountant and the thing you really need to know is I saved your life."

He smiled.

He began to walk away and I shouted,

"You forgot your hurly."

He kept on going.

I didn't have a sawn-off, least not then. I did have a second hurly.

You always have one in reserve.

19

They hit on my fourth night, a little after midnight. I was restless in the sleeping bag when two young men approached. One had a can in his hand. I feigned semiconsciousness and the first one said,

"Douse him."

I moved to the left as the liquid splashed against the wall and I was free of the sleeping bag, the hurly in my hand. I hit the first one hard across his knees and he dropped instantly, the other simply ran away.

I phoned the Guards, and to my surprise, a car arrived within minutes. Two Guards got out and I explained what had happened. They were highly suspicious of me. They took us both down to the station, the young man moaning constantly.

A new Superintendent, name of Collins, stood behind his desk, said,

"So, the infamous Jack Taylor."

There isn't a whole lot you can answer to that, so I said nothing. He asked,

"You were sleeping rough to lure the alleged assailant into attacking you?"

"Pretty much."

He made me go through the saga twice and made sounds of disapproval at every juncture.

Finally, he said,

"I won't have vigilantism on my watch, do you understand me?"

I was tired.

"Yes, sir."

He said I could go, and I asked about my hurly. He snapped,

"Evidence."

I got outside and it was raining. I sighed, feeling little sense of accomplishment.

The young man I had taken was named Tony Wren. He was fourteen years of age and came from a middle-class family. Owen, my friend in the Guards, had paid me a visit, began with,

"You might be in deep shit."

Owen looked beaten, that stage in his career when he finally realizes he is not going to make a difference. I poured him a drink and he grabbed it with relish, said,

"Thank God for Jameson."

Amen.

I asked,

"So, what am I supposed to have done?"

He emitted a long sigh, then,

"The guy you took your hurly to. His knee is completely fucked."

Good, I thought.

As if he read my mind, Owen said,

"The family are going to sue you."

What?

He reached in his jacket, took out a pack of Major, the strongest cigarette available. I said,

"You don't smoke."

He extracted one, lit it with a disposable lighter.

"I was off them for ten years, but we had a child molestation case that was extremely nasty and next thing I know, I'm back smoking."

He offered the pack, but I shook my head. He said,

"Wren's family have hired a solicitor and they are suing you."

I was only a little surprised.

"Let me guess, they say I attacked him. His buddy will back him up and it's their word against mine."

He gave a grim smile.

"Your word is that of a man sleeping on the street with the hurly. They'll massacre you in court."

He was probably right.

I offered another drink, but he reluctantly declined.

"I just wanted to give you the heads up on what's coming."

I asked,

"The other guy, his buddy, who is he?"

Owen made a bitter sound.

"A pup just a few years older than his mate."

That is not a term of endearment. In Galway it means an apprentice thug. He continued,

"His name is Scott, and he comes from money. His father designs golf courses in Dubai, so tons of cash and influence. The son had two thousand euros' worth of cocaine seized in the mail recently and the judge gave him community service. He was later on Instagram, posing on a red Porsche with what could only have been a spliff."

"Christ," I said.

Owen prepared to leave, cautioned,

"Apart from the court case, you need to watch your back, this other kid, he's a back stabber. We found a nine-length hunting knife in his room when we busted him for the coke."

I thanked him again and said I'd be careful.

⊠

The next day I got the summons from Tony Wren's solicitor. I figured I'd need to find someone to fight my side. I was beginning to get my strength back after the hospital stint and the thought of a court case, alas, did not do much for my very fragile mental state. What I most wanted was to go on an almighty skite, blow out all the stops, just do the Serenity short version, fuckit.

I had a scalding shower, drank black coffee without a shot of Jay, dressed in my 501s, a worn sweatshirt that proclaimed,

"Saw Doctors and the N17"

Pulled on a pair of Timberland boots I'd finally got comfortable with, and headed out. The day was bright, cold, and fresh, it reached your face like a whispered evocation. It felt good to be alive despite the horror of the world. Ukraine had till now held off the Russian onslaught, but the sheer number of Russian troops were gaining advantage.

I went to the GBC, old-style restaurant in the center of town. It still sold Carbohydrate Neon Nightmares with,

Fried eggs,

Sausages,

Black pudding,

Rashers (bacon),

Fried tomatoes,

Thick slices of country-style toast.

It used to be my go-to hangover cure.

I had unwittingly mentioned it to a doctor who I believed was suffering from a hangover and he'd recoiled in horror, exclaiming,

"No wonder you were in a coma."

I got a table upstairs and a warm welcome from Catherine, who'd been a waitress there for years. She used that Irish form,

"I thought you were dead."

Depending on the intonation, 'tis a compliment, but most usually an insult, as in "Wish you were."

She asked,

"The same as always?"

Which is kind of odd as I hadn't been there for coming on three years. A young man was sitting by the window, his back to me but something familiar.

He turned, went,

"Jack?"

It was Pat. He looked ten years younger and had an aura of health and zing about him. I recognize that vibe as I don't think I ever in my life had actual personal experience of it. He came over, asked,

"Might I join you?"

Fuck.

Nothing to spoil a good fry-up like a priest, especially an eager one. I said,

"Sure."

He was dressed in chinos, a dark sweater, and, I might be wrong, boat shoes. Like he'd escaped from the pages of *The Great Gatsby*.

Catherine brought over his breakfast from the window table, the remains of a salad.

Fuck again.

I stated the obvious.

"You look good."

He glowed, literally, said,

"I am now three months sober."

He reached in his pocket, took out a coin, added,

"This is my ninety-day medal."

What could I say that didn't come across as cynical, so went with the cliché,

"You deserve it."

My food arrived and he recoiled in mock horror, said,

"You can't eat that."

I gave him my long-suffering look.

"I'm going to try."

Before he could launch into a lecture, I asked,

"Are you still a priest?"

He appeared offended.

"Of course. They are very proud of me and know I can be an inspiration to others who are afflicted with this horrible disease."

He took a deep breath, and I was able to make decent inroads to my food. He said,

"There is a twelve-step program, and I know I'm a newbie, but I have decided to try and practice the eleventh step."

I didn't ask as I knew he'd continue.

He did.

"The step is about helping another alcoholic."

I said,

"Commendable."

He looked around as if somebody might eavesdrop, then announced,

"I have chosen you to be my step."

He looked like he'd delivered fantastic news, which for some it might well be, but me, not so much.

I was saved from answering straightaway by Catherine coming back. She looked at Pat, asked,

"Good Lord, Jack, is this your son?"

Phew-oh.

I said,

"He's a father."

Pause.

Let it linger, then added,

"But not to me."

She was confused so I eased up, explained,

"He's a priest and we're not related, save by drink."

She peered closely at Pat, still suspicious.

"You're awfully young to be a priest."

He smiled bashfully and I burst that bubble.

"You should have seen him three months ago; he was a bloody wreck."

Hurt him.

And I'm not even sure why, it was just nasty. I think AA talk threatens me.

Catherine moved away, with,

"Whatever you are, you're a lovely fellah."

Pat finished his salad, or whatever it was, and I offered,

"How about a strong coffee to kick-start the system?"

He looked stricken.

"I must avoid stimulants."

I wasn't sure how to answer that with anything that approached sanity. Where we were sitting, to our right, was a large bay window and you could get a clear view of the beginning of Shop Street. Pat happened to glance that way and, suddenly excited, pointed, said,

"There's my young man."

In the gay sense?

Before I could venture into that minefield, he continued,

"I have been asked to be his spiritual advisor and it is so rewarding."

With a sick feeling in my stomach, I looked more closely at the young man, the young man who was limping. Pat said,

"He had a traumatic experience recently. A homeless man he was trying to help turned on him and attacked him with a hurly."

I tried to explain to Pat that he couldn't be involved with that young man, saying the guy was bad news and to trust me, it was best to stay away. We were outside the restaurant now and Pat, surprising me, asked,

"Why should I trust you?"

Jesus.

I waffled on about me being older, more experienced in the life of the streets, and . . .

He stopped me!

Put a hand up, said,

"But you're a drunk, Jack. They told us in rehab not to enable other alcoholics and to not be afraid to confront an out-of-control alkie."

I was spitting iron, snarled,

"Alkie? You're calling me that, you fuckhead? Who stood by you when the world turned its back to you? How fucking dare you."

He smiled.

Smiled!

I very nearly walloped him but walloping a young priest on the main street of the town is never a good look. I tried to rein it in, dial back from the violence flashing through my blood, said in an almost even tone,

"I'm the homeless guy who took out his knee with a hurly."

Stopped him, but only briefly. He answered,

"But you're not homeless, Jack."

And with that, he just fucked off.

The Irish feel that confidentiality
Is really
Little more than a spiteful notion
Not to share data.

20

Ireland had now welcomed thirty thousand refugees from Ukraine. The problem was we had no place to house them. Temporary bases like large tents, arenas, were being used in a desperate effort to provide shelter.

Russia continued to bombard their country with a veritable blitzkrieg of shelling. For eight weeks, Ukraine continued to fight back.

I had to find a solicitor to defend me against the charges of assault and battery. It is generally believed, though not spoken, that if you want a good solicitor in Galway, get yourself a Protestant one, preferably with that Anglo-Irish accent.

Perhaps it is some hangover from the years of colonization, or some inbred deference to things English, but deep in our psyche we still held to the notion that, in matters of law, the Brits had an edge.

Randall Lewis Brown, there's a name not to fuck with. He had an office adjacent to the courthouse, so his location alone told you he was a shrewd cookie. I dressed to, if not impress, then at least not intimidate.

I got a fine tweed jacket in the St. Vincent de Paul shop, with a Van Heusen shirt and boat-club tie, all for twenty-five euro.

The woman serving me said,

"You'll impress somebody in that gear."

She wasn't being nasty, just observant, so I asked,

"Ah, but would I impress you?"

She gave that laugh, special to Galway women, you're never sure if the laugh is with you or about you. She said,

"But, Jack, I know you."

You don't push further.

So, thus dressed, I went to the solicitor's office. I had an appointment at twelve thirty. A secretary of the old-school type, i.e., hostile, told me to sit and be patient.

I did.

I flicked through the magazines on a table, and was vaguely considering if I might look at *Country Life*, when I was summoned. Told gravely,

"Mr. Brown will see you now."

I was ushered into the 1950s.

The office had that gray dark light of the old days, heavy furniture, and reams of solemn books, containing weighty law no doubt. Brown was in his sixties, wearing pinstripe trousers, glowing white shirt, and

Connacht Rugby tie. Heavy brogues completed the Lord of some manor image. He boomed,

"Mr. Taylor, a sherry perhaps?"

What?

He gave a chuckle, said,

"See, I read up on you. The demon drink has you by the balls if I'm to believe the press."

I was at a loss, said lamely,

"Sherry would only ever be a penance."

He liked that.

"Bravo, now tell me your pickle."

He cleared a chair of fat files for me, and I sat, began my tale of woe. He only interrupted once, to say,

"You're a modern-day Don Quixote."

When I finished, he proclaimed,

"A resounding tale."

Then he muttered to himself for a time, looked up a book, made *mmm* sounds, then eventually said,

"I do believe I can make this go away."

I hadn't expected that, asked,

"How?"

He laughed.

"Old boy's network."

"You mean Masons, Rotary Club, those kinds of boys."

He gave a satisfied smile, said,

"You know, Jack, may I call you that? Good. It's best not to know what networking really entails, just remember the word *Edge*."

I said,

"Makes me want to have a bucket of sherry."

He laughed again.

"My research on you did reveal you had a wicked sense of humor, and trust me, humor will serve you well, my friend."

He rubbed his hands together; I was being dismissed.

I got up, reached for my wallet, asked,

"Is cash, okay?"

Now he looked offended.

"This one is pro bono."

Surprised, I said,

"I am grateful."

He considered that, then,

"I may need your services in the not-too-distant future."

I was at the door, tried,

"It will also be pro bono."

He clapped me on the back.

"See, you have the gist of the old boy's network already."

21

Raftery left me a phone message, to get in touch urgently.

I did.

He said,

"Remember I told you about *Galway Confidential?*"

I said I did; I could detect mega excitement in his tone.

"Yeah, you were putting out the word on the homeless assailants on your podcast."

I added,

"That case has been resolved and I do appreciate that you tried to help."

There was a silence, then he said,

"I also asked our audience, to keep an eye out for a guy who was attacking nuns and I really expected nothing to come of that, but . . ."

I let him build the drama until he said,

"One of our listeners saw a guy behaving very oddly near the city center convent and, on a hunch, followed him. Nothing happened but he did stay on the guy's trail and wrote down the number of the car the guy was driving. A source at traffic control provided a name and an address."

I was stunned, said so.

I added,

"I owe you big time, drinks on me next time."

He said nothing for a minute, then,

"You haven't got the address from me yet."

Uh-oh.

I asked,

"Well, when can I meet you?"

I knew he wasn't giving me the data over the phone. He said,

"You intend to get the address and then deal with that on your own."

He was right. I tried to kick shape the deal.

"This is what I do, you have to trust me on that."

He gave a short, terse laugh.

"Jack, what you do is comas."

Phew-oh.

I tried to rein in a building anger.

"That's below the belt."

He chuckled, said,

"It's what you dish out regularly."

Fuck.

I caved, said,

"Okay, you can come."

I took a breath, asked,

"You want to meet at my apartment?"

He agreed.

"I'll bring the hurly, I bought one."

I said in a very controlled tone,

"Bringing a weapon and using it are two very different things. You might think it's just a matter of swinging the stick, but nigh on crushing a man's skull is a whole other gig."

I could hear him sighing. He said,

"Bit rich that you lecture me on violence."

I made a stab at easing down.

"It may not come to violence, and he may not even be the guy."

Raftery was silent and I thought he might have hung up, but then,

"He's the guy, and a fucker who attacks nuns is definitely going to need a sizable beating."

Then he hung up.

Back at my apartment, as I waited for Raftery, I took my second hurly from the cupboard. It was nearly new. I hadn't yet put the steel clips on the top but figured I could manage without them. Kept reminding myself,

"This is probably a wild-goose chase."

And yet.

I tried to read the newspapers piling up on the sofa. The photos of dead children in Ukraine were almost unbearable. It was ten days until a huge Russian celebration, the commemoration of Russia's victory in the Second World War. It was two days to May Day and Putin had hoped to have utterly conquered Ukraine by then.

He hadn't.

So, a muted May Day.

Maybe.

Putin continued to threaten the West with the nuclear option if aid was given to Ukraine.

Refugees continued to pour across Europe. Here in Ireland we had already received thirty thousand and the housing of them was a mega problem.

One-third of our own government was The Green Party, led by an ejit named Ryan. He wanted to ban the turf industry and make it illegal to sell it.

If he managed to pass this proposed bill, it was truly the end of rural Ireland.

His government partners were scathing in their criticism of him, but he refused to back down and it seemed he might yet bring down the government.

The response from the public was reminiscent of the outrage over the water charges, and that had literally brought down the previous lot.

I lit a cig, my first in three days, and was dizzy from the nicotine. I moved to the window, the bay window that revealed a brilliant view of Galway Bay.

It soothed my soul somewhat and set up that old yearning. For what, I still didn't know. My attention was drawn by a young man leaning against a bench, he was staring right at me. Something about him. . . .

Then it hit.

The two men who'd attacked the homeless, what were the names?

Yeah, Scott Williams, the one who had run away . . . and—

Tony Wren, whose knee I had shattered.

The one staring up at me, defiance writ large, was Scott Williams. It made me smile to imagine that he might have come to intimidate me. I grabbed my jacket, went down to meet him. My heart was jumping at the prospect of violence, a surge of adrenaline coursing through my veins. Outside, Williams moved from his slouch against the bench to stand up, face me. I crossed the road, got right in his face, snarled,

"You are looking for me?"

Uncertainty moved across his face, and he tried to back off a little, but the bench was blocking his passage. He was average height and I towered over him. He had regular features but odd eyes, as if they weren't in focus. He had the sort of loose body that is not quite flabby but heading fast in that direction. The sort of shape becoming common in our youth, with all the fast-food outlets and incessant phone surfing but no moving.

He summoned up something to have him say,

"I know where you live now."

I laughed into his face, spat,

"So?"

He wanted to look away, but I was so close to him that he couldn't. He said,

"So, you need to watch out."

I said,

"I'm here, let's get into it right now. Why wait?"

And I pushed him back, not very forcibly, but such was the angle, he fell over the top of the bench, landed on the prom in a tangle of limbs. I moved over, put my boot on his chest. I said,

"Look me up online and see how they heavily suggest my involvement in the deaths of fuckheads a whole lot more vicious than you could ever be."

He tried to rise but I kept him pinned. I said,

"Take this as gospel, if you ever come near my home, or me . . ."

Pause.

"Ever again, I will kill you."

I stood back and he got shakily to his feet.

"You assaulted me."

"You burned a friend of mine to death, if you think that's going away, you are even dumber than you appear. So bear in mind that, some dull evening, you'll think you've gotten away with it and you'll get a tap on the shoulder with my hurly. Your friend got his knee crushed so you can imagine what I have in mind for you."

He began very slowly to edge away from me, and tried a last hurrah, shouted,

"I'll get you!"

"You'll need more than a piss-poor attitude."

I added,

"When I was a child, if you gave cheek to an adult, they literally put a shoe in your arse, so I'm regarding your little spiel as cheek."

He looked in disbelief at me.

I put my boot in his departing arse.

Angelina Jolie visited Ukraine to, as she said, show her support, claimed she wanted it to be low-key yet somehow a flock of photographers managed to track her every move. Nancy Pelosi met with the Ukraine president, Zelensky, and promised more aid.

Zelensky did comment on . . . war tourists.

One of the remarkable things about the Ukraine refugees was their determination to bring their pets, dogs, cats, even parrots with them on their trek to freedom, turning down transport if their pets were not allowed. Arriving in Ireland, their pets were not allowed in much of the accommodation on offer.

In the UK, a Tory MP was seen watching porn in the House of Commons—twice! He claimed he'd been researching tractors on his phone.

Inflation was running rampant and the price of fuel, oil, gas rocketed. Russian TV showed a simulation where a new missile fired underwater would cause a tsunami to obliterate both Ireland and the UK. The Irish did not respond well to threats, even simulated ones.

Guinness introduced a new pint titled: *00*.

Yup, zero alcohol.

A pint of the black with no alcohol!

The country uttered a collective:

Why?

Next they'd have alcohol-free Jameson, and we'd nearly welcome a tsunami.

※

Back at my apartment, I waited on Raftery and pondered on the chances that the man we were going to visit would be the attacker of the nuns.

I was tempted to ring Sheila, tell her we might have a resolution, but knew in my bones that could go dreadfully wrong. I got my holdall ready, put the hurly in there, and poured a small Jameson, while it still had an alcohol content.

The doorbell went and I opened it to Raftery, dressed all in black. He had put a sling on his hurly and slung it on his back like a rifle or a guitar.

"You look ridiculous."

Unfazed, he came in, saw the bottle of Jay, said,

"I'll have a shot of that."

I shook my head.

"We are hoping for some discretion and looking like two wild hurlers, dressed in black, is like a neon sign."

I poured him a small Jay, said,

"You follow my lead."

He gave a tight smile.

"You seem to have confused our roles. I'm the guy with the name and address, you are in fact the tagalong."

I counted to ten, drew in a deep breath, asked,

"So, okay, who is he?"

He smiled in victory, began,

"His name is Brian Lee, works in IT, and has a house in Threadneedle Road, a handily detached house so we won't be disturbed."

I waited, He continued,

"He's single so no wife to mess with his timetable of assaulting nuns."

"Alleged," I stressed.

He stared at me.

"You don't seem too delighted we've solved this case."

My patience was now paper thin. I tried,

"We can't afford to make a mistake; we've got to get this right."

He said,

"I don't actually need you; I could go on my own, you don't know where he lives and I have a hurly. How difficult is it to swing the damn thing?"

We danced around this for a while and eventually, I said,

"Okay, let's go."

He made a mock exasperated sigh.

"Now you're talking."

Raftery was driving a white van. Said, when he caught my look at it,

"It's a crime story. Got to have a white van, or have I been reading the wrong books?"

We put the gear in the back and drove toward Threadneedle Road. We could have walked as it is but a spit from my apartment. I asked,

"Why have you a van, not a car?"

He smiled delightedly, said,

"Ah, there's the mystery."

But he didn't elaborate.

We got to the address, parked a few hundred yards from it, I reached in the back for my hold all and Raftery grabbed his hurly. I tried again.

"I think one hurly is sufficient."

He shook his head.

"Not if we're really going to wallop the hell out of the bollix."

"I desire
The things
That will
Destroy me
In the end."
   —Sylvia Plath

22

What do you say to the person whose door you knock on, the person you suspect of being a vicious attacker of nuns?

You can hardly open with asking him if he had a TV license. I reckoned I'd play it as it presents, and my main concern was Raftery. He was not only fully convinced we had the right guy but bursting to bust heads with the hurly.

I said to him again,

"You need to follow my lead and cut back on the adrenaline high."

He gave me a look, said through gritted teeth,

"You worry about yer own self fellah."

Great.

I knocked on the door, waited.

It was opened seconds later by a man in a suit and tie, looking like he was about to head for work; he was in his early forties, regular features, eyes that weren't dead but seemed to have an element of distance to them, as if something over your shoulder had his main interest. He had dark hair, cut short, streaks of gray.

He asked,

"Yes?"

I asked,

"Brian Lee?"

He nodded, his eyes resting for a moment on the hurly sticking out of Raftery's duffel bag. I said,

"I wonder if we could have a few moments of your time?"

A flash of impatience flitted over his face. He asked,

"This is not a good time, and might I inquire what exactly you wish to discuss?"

Before I could act, Raftery literally brushed me aside, launched himself at Lee, pushing his arm hard into Lee's chest, knocking him backward. He followed, pulling the hurly out and swiping Lee's legs from under him. He snarled,

"Don't play games with us, you piece of shit. We're here about you attacking nuns."

And then I got a good look at the man on the floor, grabbed Raftery, screamed,

"It's not him!"

He stopped mid-swing, asked,

"What? Of course it is."

I pointed to the man's legs, said,

"Look at his right leg, it's a goddamn prosthesis."

Raftery reeled back in shock.

"It can't be, our witness was so sure."

I leaned down, helped Lee up from the floor, tried,

"I'm terribly sorry, there has been a dreadful mistake."

Luckily, or maybe not, Lee was in too much shock to do more than nod his head.

I said,

"We'll be going now, and again, terribly sorry."

And I dragged Raftery out of there before Lee got his wits back and called the Guards. We got in the van. I took the driver's side, burned rubber out of there.

Raftery said,

"It was an honest mistake."

I glanced at him.

"Beating the shite out of an innocent man is slightly more than a mistake."

Raftery said,

"Come on, isn't it a rush just to beat some bastard, for the sheer hell of it?"

We got to my apartment, and I jumped out of the van, said,

"It would be better if I don't see you for a time."

Later, in the days of *Galway Confidential* fallout, I learned that Brian Lee was a former client of Raftery's who hadn't paid his accountancy bill and been warned,

"You'll pay but not with money."

The
    Very
        Same
            Night
                A
                    Nun
                        Was
                            Viciously
                                Attacked.

23

Sheila Winston came by, demanding to know how another attack could have occurred. I said,

"We thought we had a suspect, but it was a false alarm."

She was very angry, snapped,

"What does that even mean?"

Phew-oh.

I said,

"It means we fucked up big time."

That didn't help. She asked,

"What are you going to do now?"

I told her the truth, said,

"I've no idea."

I wanted to say the Guards had huge resources, but they had made no progress. I felt it sounded very much like an excuse.

Which it was.

I offered her coffee as a distraction.

"I'm too upset to drink coffee."

I did have Jameson but kept that thought to myself. She gave a resigned sigh, turned to leave, said,

"You've been a disappointment, Jack."

I wanted to shout,

"Like that's the first time I ever heard that!"

Randall Lewis Brown.

The solicitor with a name that rolled off the tongue like class. He phoned me, asked,

"Remember me, Mr. Taylor?"

As if I'd forget. I said I did, and he continued,

"I mentioned that we might prevail upon your services sometime in the future?"

"Yes, and I offered them pro bono."

He chuckled.

"Precisely."

I waited, then he said,

"We have a matter of some delicacy we need amending."

Amending!

What a splendid term, covered all kinds of nefarious activities, and delivered in his baritone Anglo-Irish, you could almost look forward to it.

Almost.

He said,

"One of the partners in our little firm is being pressured by a predatory young lady and we'd like her to go away."

I nearly laughed, asked,

"In the American sense of the term?"

He was horrified, near shouted,

"Good Lord, no, we don't do that, least not outside of a courtroom. You gave me a turn there, Mr. Taylor."

I waited for more. He continued,

"Her name is Sheila Winston."

Fuck and fuck again.

He took my stunned silence as some form of assent, continued,

"Let's meet and I'll give you the details. We don't want to discuss this on an open line."

I didn't want to discuss it at all, but he went on,

"Let's meet at my club."

He had a club.

Course he had; he was Anglo.

"Where is it?"

He chuckled, said,

"Sorry, how could you possibly know?"

There's the thing, when you're insulted by an accent, it doesn't seem so bad. Maybe it's a genetic hand-me-down after five hundred years of insults.

He said,

"The Codicil is located at the rear of the courthouse, number ninety-one, and you'll appreciate this, there is no number ninety or indeed ninety-two."

And this seemed to amuse him greatly. It made no sense but perhaps it's legal humor.

He asked,

"Are you free round seven this evening?"

I said I was, and he added,

"Wear a suit."

That didn't sound better in any accent.

I did wear a suit, if one from a charity shop still qualified.

The shirt, a Ben Sherman, also from the charity outlet, a Galway United tie, and my Doc Martens. Difficult to wear the Docs anymore as the fashionistas had discovered them and are issuing them in every shape and color under a trendy sun.

I hadn't shaved for a few days so let the father of Jason Statham look remain. I was good to go.

Found the club without too much difficulty, was confronted by a heavy oak door with a bronze knocker in the shape of a gavel. What the

Americans might term cute. The door was opened, sounding like heavy bolts being withdrawn, and there stood a very large man in a suit not unlike my own.

"Yes?"

I was very tempted to ask him if he'd been to my charity shop, but sometimes, you just must let the good lines slide. I said,

"My name is Jack Taylor and I believe I'm expected."

I didn't say by whom.

Why should I do all the work?

He moved back, a lectern behind him with a heavy-duty ledger on it. He flipped a page, said,

"You're late."

"Story of my life," I tried.

He moved aside, said,

"Go down the stairs, wait to be seated."

I did.

Brown was sitting in a well-worn leather armchair and another empty one faced him. He beckoned me. Of the many things that irritate me, being beckoned is in my top ten. I ambled over, no hurry, and he indicated I should sit. An elderly waiter appeared beside me; I mean he literally seemed to come out of the woodwork. Why are these club retainers/butlers always centuries old?

Brown said,

"Mr. Taylor will have a G and T."

I looked at the waiter, his expression was one of mild contempt if he could be bothered to assess me at all. I said,

"Mr. Taylor will have a Jameson, double, no ice."

Brown gave a tight smile.

"G and Ts are the preferred beverage of the club."

I gave him an even tighter smile.

"But I'm not of the club, am I?"

His face said,

And never will be.

We sat in silence, awaiting the controversial Jameson, not so much surveying each other as biding our time. Brown was in what I hazard might pass as casual wear for the club.

He had loosened his tie and his waistcoat was open, revealing a hefty stomach, straining against the buttons of what might wonderfully have been a Ben Sherman shirt. My drink came and, yes, on a silver tray. I took it, muttered,

"Ta."

As pig-ignorant as it sounds.

I raised my glass as Brown raised his, and he toasted,

"Cheers, pip pip."

Pip?

I said,

"Sláinte."

He smiled at me. If a lawyer smiles at you, head for the hills. He said,
"I've been working on your case."

And waited.

I think I was meant to show gratitude, so I went,

"Great."

He laughed.

"Not a ringing endorsement, but righty-oh, let's not dwell on bad
manners. I've been in touch with the plaintiff's legal team, and they
agreed to back off. I think the mention of a man being burnt to a crisp
by their client did sway their decision and, without blowing my own
trumpet too much, they know I'm a fucking Rottweiler in court."

The f-word was so unexpected that I nearly dropped my glass. He
was happy with that reaction and continued,

"Now, the matter to hand."

He reached for a battered briefcase that had his initials on the front,
rummaged in there, said,

"Oh, I forgot to eat my lunch."

And flipped a bacon roll on to the table.

Whatever I felt about him and liking him was never part of it, he
was entertaining. He raised his hand, a gold Rolex sliding elegantly
along his wrist, and the waiter/butler appeared. He said to him,

"Another round, my good fellow."

As I said, entertaining.

He placed a yellow legal pad on the table, glanced through it, then
looked at me.

"Thing is, Taylor, as I might have said, one of my colleagues finds himself in a bit of a pickle."

I nodded as if pickle was a normal part of my world. He continued,

"This . . ."

Paused.

"A woman was involved with my legal partner, they had their moment in the sun, and he ended it but she is not dissuaded. She feels she has been used and wants to tell my friend's wife and generally make a bit of a scandal."

I echoed,

"He is married?"

And got the look from him. He downed the freshly arrived drink, gulped, snapped,

"Is that a problem?"

"Not for me," I said.

"Ted, Teddy as we know him, Edward Deauville of the Ougherard Deauvilles, wishes this to all go away, for her to go away, and is prepared to pay her a not unreasonable sum to do so."

Phew-oh.

I drank my Jameson, it had ice in it, the heresy of that. I said,

"I know her."

He looked startled, recovered.

"Splendid, maybe you can persuade her to desist in her folly without any financial recompense."

I doubt it.

I continued,

"The money will only annoy, not to mention insult, her, and she has a streak of stubbornness that might prove difficult."

He waved this away as if it were so much trivial nonsense.

"Make the offer, she'll jump at it. And of course, we'll need it in writing that she won't bother us further."

I was almost amazed at his naïveté, leaned over to get his full attention, said,

"This is not a woman who'll respond well to threats and God only knows how she'll react to an offer of money."

He seemed to consider, then,

"You seem to have confused our roles a tad. I tell you what I want and you . . ."

Pause.

"You deliver."

You fucking believe it?

He finished his drink, belched, said,

"I saved you from a trial that might have put you in jail, so I expect some loyalty."

I was lost for words, least any words that didn't contain many expletives. I stood up, said,

"Thank you for the drinks."

He gave me a radiant smile.

"Get it done, asap, there's a good chap."

"You don't have to say anything,
Always remember that.
Many a person
Has missed the opportunity
To say nothing
And lost much
Because of it."

—From the film: *An Cailín Ciúin*

(*The Quiet Girl*)

24

When I am in a mental quandary, which is often, and shots of Jay only confuse me, I go to the movies. Two hours of pure escape.

I went to see *An Cailín Ciúin* (*The Quiet Girl*) which is ninety minutes of heart-aching bliss. A movie of pure simplicity that might well be among the most powerful events I have witnessed.

I came out the cinema shattered and now I needed shots of Jay.

A young woman looked at me, went,

"How-r-yah, Jack?"

Took me a moment, then I realized she was Clare Anne Irwin, daughter of Galway's most celebrated undertaker. She had been recently crowned the Galway Rose, and unlike the other competitors, she had a profession that was as rare as it was misunderstood. She loved being a mortician and had fought stiff opposition from men at every stage of her career.

She brought a lightness and, yes, even a true feeling of comfort to a profession not noted for those qualities.

I said,

"Congrats on your win."

She was delighted, asked again how I was.

You really don't want to tell an undertaker you're not feeling well so I lied almost convincingly. She told me it was good to see me, and you know, I walked away with a lighter tread.

I arranged to meet with Sheila Winston in the lobby of the Great Southern Hotel. Now known as The Hardiman. We were to meet at noon, and if the event went well, we might even have lunch.

Fuck.

I dreaded what I was going to ask/tell her and ran various scenarios in my head, but they all came to the same end: stop harassing the man.

She arrived on time, dressed in a light blue blazer and gray jeans. She looked well but I was about to mess that up. She gave me a hug, said,

"I'm glad to see you."

Right.

A waiter came and we ordered a pot of coffee, and she sat back in her chair, asked,

"So, what is the news, Jack? Raftery told me ye were close to catching the attacker."

Gave me some time and I gave her the long version of how we didn't catch the guy, but we were still hopeful.

The coffee came like a brief reprieve. I poured, took a sip, sat forward.

She said,

"What's going on, Jack?"

I told her how I'd been using the lawyer, Brown, to deal with the allegations against me and how he'd managed to make the charges disappear.

She clapped her hands.

"Oh, that is great news, Jack."

Uh-oh.

I said,

"Thing is, they'd like if you would cease all communication with one of their partners."

There, I'd said it, in all its bare, brutal case.

I waited.

She had her coffee cup in her hand, and I could see the debate on her face . . . Throw it, or no?

She put the cup down.

"For a moment there, I wanted to scald you."

I tried,

"I know it's a shock but probably for the best."

She had her hand up, snarled,

"For the best? The fuck does you know what's for the best?"

I said,

"I know the guy is married, and how is that going to work?"

She was scarlet from anger.

"His marriage is a sham; he's getting a divorce."

And she started to weep. I offered a tissue, but she slapped my hand away.

"Don't you dare feel pity for me."

I offered,

"Maybe a drink, a brandy?"

She composed herself, literally shook herself, sneered,

"The Jack Taylor solution to everything."

Low.

She stood up, rooted in her bag, flung a rake of notes on the table, said,

"You've been paid."

I hung my head, and she had a parting shot.

"Try a brandy."

25

I met Owen Daglish in Busker Brownes, famous for its Sunday morning jazz sessions. I'd been meaning to go for years but Sunday mornings usually found me trying to recover from something.

Owen looked tired, the situation with the refugees from Ukraine was putting a strain on the Guards.

I'd ordered him a pint and the barman were just creaming the head of it when Owen sat down. He said,

"The force just got five hundred new recruits, of all nationalities. It is becoming a multiracial outfit."

I told him about the tip from *Galway Confidential* that led us to thinking we might catch the nun attacker. He put his pint down, gave me a strange look, and I asked,

"What?"

He shook his head, asked,

"What's *Galway Confidential*?"

I thought he was joking but he wasn't.

"It's a very popular podcast with more than twenty thousand listeners."

He signaled to the barman to fix up fresh pints, then turned to me, said

"There's no such thing."

Galway Confidential didn't exist and the shock of that led me to question everything. Just who the hell was Raftery and what was his game? I knew nothing about him. I had taken literally everything he told me on trust.

And where did that leave his story of *Galway Confidential* knowing who the nun assailant was? It was all lies. The main question being *why?* I was in my apartment a few days later and the doorbell went. I opened it to Raftery. He came in and I was friendly, poured him a drink, let him get comfortable, then asked,

"How is *Galway Confidential* going?"

He had but a moment of doubt but that moved fast on his face, and he said,

"Good, the figures are up so that will lead to new advertising."

Jesus.

I asked,

"Where is it located on the wavelength? Give me the coordinates so I can listen."

He looked at me, assessed the situation.

"Why now, Jack? You never showed a whole load of interest before."

I said in a neutral tone,

"You're my good friend, sat by my bed when I was in a coma, you're always there for me so the least I can do is show an interest. Like, where do you live?"

He was sitting facing me, and within the space of a few minutes his whole appearance altered. The bonhomie was replaced by an expression of pure ice, his eyes were like granite. He put his glass carefully on the table, said,

"Time to back the fuck off now, Jack."

I was on my feet, bewildered, tried,

"Who the hell are you?"

He said,

"Ah, Jack, I had hoped the charade could last a little longer, least until I killed the last of the nuns."

Floored me.

I fumbled for words, and he reached for the bottle of Jay, poured me a measure, handed it to me, and in shock, I simply took it, downed it. He said,

"The day on the bridge, when the lunatic stabbed you, it was a revelation to me, I'd saved a life. Especially then, as I was planning my campaign against the nuns. So, I began to visit you, you'd piqued my fascination. Then you came out of the coma, and the whole situation, it was such a mind fuck, I stayed with it. *Galway Confidential* is something I thought might fly so I ran it by you, and you bought it absolutely."

Of all the things I could have asked I began with the biggest.

"Why are you killing nuns?"

He poured himself a drink, began,

"I could give you a sad convoluted story of childhood abuse, throw in a Magdalene laundry reference, but the truth is, I like it. It's so wonderfully blasphemous. The thing is now, Jack, what are you going to do?"

Maybe it was the Jay or shock, but I said,

"I'm going to bury you."

He laughed as he asked,

"What might you put on my headstone?"

I said,

"Galway Confidential."

"Who can you tell, Jack? I mean, it's a crazy story and your credibility is never high. Plus, the evidence for me being your best mate is all there."

With that, he turned to leave, added,

"Nun but the brave."

And was gone.

He was right—who'd believe me? I phoned Sheila and had to fast say,

"Don't hang up."

"Better be good."

"It's about the nuns."

She told me she was down at The Claddagh, walking along the shoreline, and she'd meet me there. I got my Garda coat, headed out. I spotted her down near Nimmo's Pier and walked to meet her. She was dressed for wind-walking and her face had that healthy glow that comes in from the bay. She was not pleased to see me.

I said,

"I think we should sit down for this."

She didn't.

There was no easy way to tell it, so I began,

"I know who attacked the nuns."

"You've solved it."

I wanted the glory, course I did, but I told her the truth, said,

"Not exactly, the attacker told me."

She said,

"I need to sit down."

We found a vacant bench along the pier, we sat, and she looked at me with something like rage.

"Just tell me."

So I did.

I went through the whole scenario and how, when I confronted Raftery, he literally just told me. Her face was a riot of horror, fright, anger, confusion, and she went,

"Why?"

I wished I had some pat answer, but the truth was he did it because he wanted to. Why did he want to? Because he was an evil bastard.

When I had finished, I waited for her response, she was silent for ages, just staring out at the swans. A mother swan was trailing her cygnets in a straight line, a picture of beauty and even peace.

Finally, Sheila spoke,

"There's one thing to do now."

I was about to lay out how going to the Guards was a waste of time without evidence, but before I could start my lame litany, she said,

"You are going to kill him."

Keeping something confidential
In Galway
Means you only
Tell two people
Instead of three.

26

Two cases of Monkey Pox reported in Ireland.

A weary public asked,

"What fresh hell is this?"

I had gotten to know the street people during my brief time with them and an unlikely bond had developed. Three men, who had lasted over a decade living below the radar, seemed to believe I was but a drink away before I ended up full time on the streets.

They had shouted this to me one evening as I left a parcel of supplies with them, and something clicked in my head, madness or no. I told them of Scott Williams, one of the two young guys who'd killed their compadre. They listened in silence then asked about the other one. I said he was attempting to bring me to court but that Williams had told me he would deal with me personally. That last bit interested them most and one said,

"Did he now?"

They offered me a slug of their perennial Buckfast, but I declined, it kicks like be damned.

A few days later, Scott Williams was fished out of the dock, a tragic accident the papers said. I later learned from Owen Daglish that the only item found on Scott Williams, body was a bottle of Buckfast. Owen had looked at me, asked,

"Why would a rich kid like that be drinking rot gut?"

Why indeed?

Tony Wren, the other assailant, who'd attempted to bring me to court, left town and no one was willing to divulge where he might be headed. If he came back, he might well be drinking Buckfast too. I don't know if justice was in any way done with those two psychos but at least they were off the board.

Raftery went to ground. I never knew exactly where he lived as he'd been vague on that info, and now when I investigated him, he was a ghost. People knew him vaguely, but nobody had any definite knowledge of him.

Sheila had come around to my apartment, and she was not happy.

"How can you not know where he lives?"

I tried,

"Hey, I was in a coma for two years and he was the first person I saw."

She glared at me, said,

"He was your friend. He seemed to be always in your company."

I gave up, I had nothing.

She examined me from head to toe.

"I can't believe I used to think you had some character."

She produced a very heavy rosary, the beads seemed to be pearls and the cross appeared to be of solid gold. She said,

"This dates from the seventeenth century and was blessed by Padre Pio."

I nearly said,

"Your version of worry beads, and God knows you've plenty to worry on."

But I said,

"Impressive."

Which it was.

She held it in her hands, her eyes seeing something ethereal. She said,

"When you apprehended the monster attacking our nuns, we were going to present it to you."

What could I say? I said nothing.

She sighed.

"But not now of course."

She asked again about the Guards, and I told her that Raftery's confession to me was hearsay and my credence with them was never too strong.

I said,

"He'll show up. All of this is like unfinished business to him and one thing I do know is he has a sense of arrogance and—"

She stopped me mid-flow, snapped,

"Talk, speculation, that's all you've got. If he does show up, I won't be anticipating your dealing with him."

As she left, she said,

"The nuns aren't praying for you anymore."

The shame of it.

I was walking down Shop Street, and wondering where the ton of people were coming from. A guy I knew vaguely from a pub I was once barred from saw me, said,

"It's pride."

I had no reply to that, so he continued,

"LGBT and other initials I don't know."

I watched as a rainbow of color and outrageous fashion passed by. The guy asked me,

"What'cha make of that, huh?"

I said,

"It's certainly colorful."

I knew he was hoping for some rant or insulting commentary, but before I could reply, through the crowd, on the far side of the street, I glimpsed Raftery. He was but a fleeting flicker and then he was gone. I went after him.

Had to fight through the crowd, and by the time I got to the other side, there was no sign. Did I imagine him?

I made my way up the street, turned into Dominic Street, my heart pounding.

What would I do if I caught up with him?

A citizen's arrest.

The problem with that was, I never was, and was unlikely to be, a citizen.

The next time I heard
About the black pearl
Rosary beads
Was when the coroner
Described how it was used to strangle
Sheila Winston.

27

I was deep in sleep, enduring a nightmare about *Roe v. Wade.*

It involved priests, women with bloody placards, dead babies, and a nun screeching at me about where I stood on the above amendment, I don't know what, if anything, I answered.

Such was the force of the dream and the pounding on the door that I fell out of the bed. I cursed like a trooper, pulled on a T-shirt that had a faded logo for The Red Hot Chili Peppers, and struggled into my 501s, muttering,

"This better be something epic."

And opened the door . . . to Father Pat.

I presumed he was out there doing priestly gigs in a sober fashion.

Wrong.

He fell into my apartment, reeking of booze, shouting,

"What took you so long to answer?"

I took a deep breath, counted to ten.

Then I punched him in the gut.

He didn't vomit all over me but simply sank to his knees with a surprised sigh. I went to make some coffee and could hear him muttering prayers as he tried to rise from the floor. I got my coffee, went and sat on the sofa and waited. The coffee was good, black, bitter with a nasty kick. I debated throwing half in Pat's face.

He finally managed to get to his feet, tried,

"I'm sorry, Jack."

"You're not sorry, you're an alkie. You're full of self-pity, but sorry you aren't."

He mumbled,

"I'm sorry about Miss Winston."

What?

I stared at him, snarled,

"What about her?"

He looked frightened, as well he should. I felt homicidal rage building. He was almost too fearful to answer but managed,

"She was found dead this morning; it was on the news."

Christ Almighty.

I asked how but I knew in my heart the answer. Pat eyed me nervously, said,

"They suspect foul play."

I nearly laughed. Foul play, too fucking right.

My TV was on behind Pat and Sky News was reporting on yet another shooting in the US. The shooter had been captured and was as now almost mandatory, an eighteen-year-old white male.

Pat was shuffling his feet, said,

"Did you hear Boris Johnson resigned as prime minister?"

I had no sane reply to that. The world was just so utterly broken.

I was up to my arse in nuns.

Can you say that?

Probably not.

The Mother Superior had summoned me. And you can guess that being summoned is not on my list of favorite activities. The last thing I'd heard was that the nuns were no longer praying for me. Father Pat had delivered the summons, on his first day of not drinking since his relapse.

I was in no mood for nuns or indeed for Pat, snapped,

"No."

He was confused, asked,

"How do you mean?"

I thought it was clear and concise, but then, he was in a twenty-four-hour blitz of alcohol withdrawal, and I knew how that goes. So I practiced patience, said,

"No means I won't go see the Mother Superior."

I did go.

Out of curiosity and to pay my respects for the death of Sheila Winston too. The convent was bathed in sunshine. A more fervent soul might have said,

"God shone His Light."

I saw an uncommonly fine day; my time of miracles was long past. A young nun answered my knock, invited me in, offered refreshments, and the devil was in me to ask for a large Jameson, no ice. But with nuns, who knows? I'm sure there was Jameson on the premises, probably stored in a wood barrel in the basement.

I was told to sit, and the Mother Superior would be with me shortly. There was a large picture of the Madonna, and a caption identified her as *Our Lady of Galway.*

That was news to me, I didn't know we'd our own personal Lady. Go figure.

The convent was quiet, not an oppressive silence but a calm comfortable absence of noise, something that was nicely soothing. No wonder nuns looked so Zen.

The young nun returned, said I could now enter the office on my left.

I did.

The Mother Superior greeted me formally with,

"Mr. Taylor."

I tried,

"Call me Jack."

She didn't.

I asked her how I should address her?

She conceded that Kate would be fine.

Seemed odd to me, but then how normal is sitting before a Mother Superior, an abbess, ever going to be?

I gave it a shot, ventured,

"Kate, my deepest sympathy on the loss of Sheila."

A silence hovered over us for what seemed ages, then she said,

"Sheila was a wonderful human being."

I agreed, waited.

She continued,

"She had tremendous faith in you."

She didn't say it but the tone of disbelief inherent in the phrasing was plain. I said,

"I am so sorry we didn't get a resolution, but we do know who the perpetrator is."

Kate, looking me full in the face, asked,

"And are you near to catching him?"

When in a tight spot, bluster.

"I'm sure 'tis but a matter of time."

Lame, right?

She said,

"You have no idea really."

She sighed, changed tack, said,

"The great love of Sheila's life was Trip."

I wasn't sure I'd heard right, echoed,

"Trip, like to travel?"

She nearly smiled, said,

"Trip is, was, her shih tzu."

Fuck.

I had a frightening premonition of where this was going and I tried to cut it off, said,

"I have a bad history with dogs."

She smiled, said,

"And you have such a wonderful track record with people."

She stood up, business concluded, went,

"Sister May is waiting in the hall with Trip. You'll be pleased to know a leash, dog bowl, treats, rubber bones are all neatly packed for you two."

I made up my mind, no way was I being railroaded, or is that dog railed?

I said,

"Ain't happening, Sister."

Injected as much hard into it as you'd allow for a nun. I can do hard-ass. Kate brushed past me, said,

"Don't be ridiculous, the dog is waiting, and I have a convent to run."

And she was gone.

I headed for the door, and sure enough, there was Sister May with the dog and a holdall. She handed me the leash and the dog looked at me with what appeared to be contempt.

Boris Johnson finally resigned as prime minister, after near sixty MPs deserted him. His resignation speech outside No. 10 was full of bluster and seemed more like a victory speech than a resignation.

This meant that the Northern Irish Protocol might yet be saved, though, as the dreaded 12th of July rolled up, the orange order burned two hundred fifty bonfires throughout the province. Some hatred just didn't want to die.

A heat wave raged through Europe, with temperatures reaching forty degrees. Massive fires in France, Spain, Portugal continued for days.

We had three days of the heat wave, the highest temp reaching thirty-three degrees, leaving the country in a state of utter befuddlement. We just don't do heat.

We now had forty thousand refugees from Ukraine and the scarcity of accommodation resulted in hundreds of refugees having to sleep on the floor of Dublin airport.

Inflation was out of control and every day brought new warnings of shortages of fuel, petrol, energy.

I sat in my apartment, the dog sitting in front of me, his head cocked to the side. I said,

"I'm all you've got."

28

Raftery watched Jack Taylor walking a dog.

A dog?

When did that happen?

And to Raftery's amusement, it seemed like it was a *Shits Su*. He figured that was how you'd pronounce the dog's breed. He would have thought Taylor would have a Rottweiler at the very least.

Go figure.

Raftery knew he'd have to kill Taylor, but he was in no hurry. Truth was, he liked the guy. Seemed like aeons ago when he'd been crossing the Wolfe Tone Bridge and witnessed a guy plunging a knife repeatedly into Taylor's body.

Without much reflection, he'd picked the attacker up and flipped him over the bridge. The guy didn't drown but you can't win 'em all.

He'd begun visiting Taylor in the hospital because it amused him that he'd saved the dude's life.

It was round the time he'd begun attacking nuns.

Were the two events connected?

He didn't know or care a whole lot. Raftery had only ever loved one person, his sister, Jenny. As children, they'd been orphaned at a young age and Jenny had been banished to one of the few remaining infamous Magdalene laundries.

Jenny had run away many times, and on her third attempt, she'd killed herself. Raftery, in a comfortable foster home, had gone berserk, and in truth, a few years were literally lost to him as he endured mental hospitals, jails, various beatings, and the one figure who stalked each nightmare, real and imagined, was the figure of a nun.

The nun who'd told him of Jenny's suicide.

Raftery knew that attacking a nun, despite the anticlerical mood of the country, was still going to be a shocker. Attack a whole series of them and you have a whole feature of shock.

But Sheila Winston was a special case, he felt true hate for her. She resented Raftery's friendship with Jack Taylor and was forever interfering in their narrative. She had questioned his claim of being Jack's brother, and to make matters worse, she ensured Taylor was hired to investigate the nun attacks.

The black rosary beads.

He remembered the day she showed him the beads. She'd said,

"This is for Jack when he solves the attacks."

There and then, he'd nearly snatched them from her, shouted,

"Guess what, you just solved it."

But wait.

He could do waiting; it sweetened the deed if there'd been a time of anticipation. When the time came, he simply asked her if he might examine the beads and she just handed them over.

No fuss, he'd wrapped them round her neck, put his boot in her back, and pulled like a bastard.

There was a time in Ireland when . . .

Confidential

Implied:

You had something to hide.

Now, it was suspected . . .

It meant:

You won the lottery.

29

Raftery seemed to have gone to ground. Speaking of ground, I had been to Charlie Byrne's and picked up a debut novel, titled,

Old Country.

By two brothers.

It was the first novel I'd been able to read as my concentration had been fucked by the coma. I'd often said that books saved my sanity, and indeed, perhaps my life. There's always been books in my bedraggled history and the fear of losing the gift of reading was just one more fear.

The dog, Trip, sat in front of me, the leash at his paws. I said,

"Cute trick."

And it worked. I had bought him a new collar, dark blue, and as I fitted it on him now, he wagged his tail. Not a wild enthusiasm but a certain contained joy. It had occurred to me to read up on his breed, but I figured that the best method of knowing this creature was literally hands-on.

I put some treats in the back pocket of my jeans and I swear the dog gave a knowing nod, like,

"You're doing good."

I was wearing my 501s, my Doc Martens, black T-shirt that had a faded photo of Rory Gallagher. The weather was poised for a promised heat wave so no jacket required.

We got outside and for a moment I thought I saw Raftery leaning against a car outside the new cinema on the Salthill prom. But it was momentary, and I dismissed it, knowing a degree of paranoia was fueling a lot of my mind's chicanery.

Sheila had obviously taught the dog well as I'd no problem guiding him on the lead. A woman stopped and,

Oh-ah.

Trip took it in his stride, and over the next thirty minutes, I realized what a babe magnet the dog was. In truth, I let the whole image down. If the dog owner had matched the magnetism of the dog, we'd have been elected.

How it goes.

We got down on the edge of the beach, dogs were forbidden on the actual beach for the summer months. The rubbish left on the sand by the public daily would shame a dog. I threw a stick and croaked,

"Fetch."

Feeling slightly ridiculous.

Trip looked at the stick, then at me, and his expression said,

"Seriously, you think I'm running after that?"

A man in his late sixties was passing, asked,

"You do know dogs are not allowed on the beach during the summer months?"

Infuriated me. I snapped,

"Do you see the dog on the sand? Does he have as much as a paw touching it?"

The man began to back off, the look on his face showing he'd touched a hornets' psycho nest. I said,

"You missed the memo on the whole mind factor."

He stopped, interested but cautious, tried,

"I'm not familiar with that."

"Yeah," I said, "it's kind of an old idea, but basically it means, mind your own fucking business."

This came out way sharper, rougher than I intended but he scarpered sharpish. The dog looked at me with what might have been a new level of respect.

We continued our walk with a spring in our respective steps.

Back at my apartment, I was putting down Trip's bowl of nuts when the doorbell went. I opened it to a tall muscular man with a shaved head, in his midfifties, he was dressed in combat trousers, thick boots, body T-shirt, a sleeve tattoo covered his right arm.

Everything about him shouted army, well, somebody's army.

"Jack Taylor?"

I nodded and he put out a thick, heavily calloused hand. He said,

"I'm Quinlan."

I didn't ask him in. He asked,

"May I come in?"

I gave a bitter chuckle.

"Really, I don't know you."

I was remembering Raftery's story of his Marine buddy.

He rubbed his head, looked tired for a moment.

"Raftery didn't mention me?"

The dog sniffed at the man's legs, then began to wag his tail.

I said,

"Come in."

He filled the apartment with his bulk, seemed to realize that, tried,

"I have trouble fitting in, so to speak."

I waited and he took a full scan of the room, said,

"You've got the whole Zen gig going."

Bollix.

"Naw, I'm just poor."

He enjoyed that, then asked,

"What do you know about Raftery?"

I told the truth.

"Absolutely nothing."

"How can that be?"

I sighed, answered,

"Try being in a coma for two years, you come to, and are told a man not only saved your life but visits every day. You think what? I'm going to ask for his CV?"

He laughed, said,

"Aye, I heard you were sharp."

I asked,

"How did you find me?"

He gave a wry smile, said,

"You must be the easiest person in this city to find. When I read about nuns being killed, I knew it had to be Raftery, so I came here, and lo and behold, everyone I ask tells me about the hero who saved your life. I got your address on Google search."

I was tiring of him.

"You want to get to the point, any point at this stage?"

He gave me a full look, the one that suggests there might be more to you than hitherto appeared. (I have yearned for many a barren year to use *hitherto*.)

He asked,

"Might I trouble you for a dram?"

He was Scottish, perhaps.

"I could maybe stretch for a whiskey but it's Irish."

He laughed again, echoed,

"Is there any other kind?"

So, not Scottish.

I poured two solid measures, handed one over, said,

"Sláinte."

He winked at me.

You believe it? A fucking wink.

I hadn't smoked a cigarette in months but just then an overriding urge for nicotine assailed me. I rooted in the press, found a pack of Major, the real coffin nails, and my battered Zippo. I lit one up and felt that treacherous joy. I looked at Quinlan, offered the pack, he debated for all a moment, uttered,

"Aw, fuckit."

Took one and I fired him up. He didn't cough on the inhale and those cigs are the original mule kick, so not his first rodeo. I asked,

"You've drank my booze, smoked my cigs, so I think it really is past time for some sort of yarn from you."

He moved to the sofa, drink in one hand, cig in the other, the picture of contentment, began,

"I was in the Forces with Raftery. You don't need to know which Force save the one that paid well for special skills."

I waited.

"We left that gig round about the same time for an opportunity to work as special security for VIPs in Afghanistan. Raftery liked to select a random civilian and claim he was a terrorist. He didn't care if they were, he just liked to beat the shit out of people."

I remembered Brian Lee and his prosthesis.

Quinlan stopped, looked for an ashtray, I gave him a saucer and he ground out the cig, said,

"I enjoyed that."

He indicated he meant the cig, I nodded and waited. He said,

"The pay was terrific, but the work was hazardous in the extreme."

He stopped, his eyes sunk in his head for a minute, then he shook himself, continued,

"Some guys can deal with the high-octane tension on a twenty-four/seven basis and Raftery seemed to thrive on the knife edge of adrenaline. I burned out after a year and change but Raftery did two tours, it's a junkie speed record. When Raftery finally bailed, he looked me up, we'd stayed in touch via email and he asked if he might crash at my place. I was living in London, trying to figure out my next life move. He was older, of course, and there was a quietness about him that didn't speak of any kind of peace. I was drinking a lot then and he seemed more than willing to match me drink on drink. But come a certain time of the evening, it was like a darkness came into his eyes and he'd mutter, 'I hate fucking nuns.' It shocked the shit out of me the first few times, and then he'd say he had to go, hunt something."

Quinlan took a deep breath, said,

"After a week, he lit out. No goodbye, just gone."

I wasn't sure what to say to this, but he wasn't finished.

"Raftery was always a whiz of technology and he used that to clean out my bank accounts."

Fuck.

He stared at me, asked,

"I was supposed to be his buddy, imagine what he might have done if he disliked me?"

I asked him,

"Why are you here?"

He spread his arms wide.

"To buddy up, catch this muttah-fuckah together."

I nearly laughed, went with,

"No, I don't really do buddies, and the time or two I did, it ended very badly."

He was surprised, tried,

"You're no match for him alone."

I let that linger, then,

"I'll find him."

He stood up, took out a card, said,

"That's got my cell on there. Call anytime but be best all round if you let me worry about Raftery."

"I'm not worried."

He chuckled, said,

"Then you know even less about Raftery than I figured."

Another scorching heat wave arrived, twenty-five degrees and rising. This for Ireland was incredible but within days people were bitching, *It's too hot!*

I couldn't bring the dog out as the pavements were too hot. I kept him hydrated and he seemed content to lounge at home. I felt he was maybe getting used to me, but I also felt we had a way to travel before he might like me.

The Mother Superior summoned me.

I doubted she had further employment in mind but went along anyway, I was wearing a light pair of French Connection jeans which I'd picked up at the charity shop, plus some Under Armour T-shirts. I really wanted to go barefoot or even sandals, but sandals, yeah, like fuck.

The same young nun answered the door of the convent.

"You're becoming quite the regular visitor."

These nuns were not short of opinions. I said,

"I was summoned."

And she laughed,

"Aren't we all?"

I stood before the Mother Superior, feeling like I was in front of the teachers of my youth. Without looking up, she indicated I sit. I had a choice of a soft-looking couch or a hard-backed chair. I took the latter, figuring I'd stay with the hard choices.

She looked up, asked,

"Why the hard option?"

I nearly laughed.

"Is this an interrogation, a sort of door A or door B?"

She sat back, smiled, and what a difference it made to her appearance, took years away from her strong face. I noticed a statue I hadn't seen before, said,

"That's Saint Anthony?"

She nodded.

"You have an affinity for that saint?"

"There used to be a small shop in Forster Street that dealt in knick-knacks and religious icons. I went in there to get a statue of Saint Martin."

She interjected,

"Saint Martin, Good Lord."

"Saint Martin and the reason I needed him is a whole other story, and not for today, but anyway, I asked the proprietor, a chancer named Davis, if he had a small replica of Saint Martin."

He confirmed he had and presented me with a replica of Saint Anthony.

She laughed again so I continued,

"I told him it was Saint Anthony and he told me I had some cheek, not only disparaging Saint Martin, but Anthony too."

She said,

"You have your moments, Mr. Taylor."

She studied me carefully and I wondered how she felt about French Connection. I noticed her examine my Doc Martens. I said,

"They have steel toe caps."

Why, why on God's earth, did I share that? I mean, come on, really, with a mother superior.

Call it nerves.

She surprised me by saying,

"Birkenstocks are making an unexpected stir in the fashion world, probably due to the pandemic, when it didn't matter what your footwear looked like. I mean, who'd see them?"

I had nothing, truly nothing. A mother superior is a fashionista?

She gave a nervous laugh, said,

"I obviously had too much time on my hands recently."

Made me like her a bit more.

She stood up, went to a room to her right, commanded,

"Follow me, Mr. Taylor."

I did.

To a small kitchen. She went to a fridge in the corner, took out two bottles of Galway water, said,

"Sláinte."

The bottle was ice cold, perfect.

"Thank you."

She headed back to her office, said,

"Manners? You can't beat them."

She continued,

"I gather you'd appreciate the water more if it had a drop of Jameson."

I nearly laughed, answered,

"You seem to be well informed on me."

She gave me that long clerical look, where nothing good is coming down the pike.

"I googled you."

This really made me laugh. I said,

"Next, you'll be playing video games."

And she laughed.

"Don't rule it out."

"I'd give a lot to witness that."

She waved a hand, dismissing all this chitchat, said,

"We'd like to reemploy you."

I went,

"Ah."

She produced an envelope, said,

"I think you'll find we have been very generous in our estimation of your time."

And suddenly wanting to fuck with her, asked,

"And my worth, how'd you reckon that?"

Her face changed, the expression now explained why she was the head honcho. She said,

"Please don't try my patience."

My name was written on the front, in a beautiful gothic script.

I said,

"Beautiful handwriting."

She gave a small tight smile, said,

"I was taught by nuns."

"A dying art," I said and could have bitten my tongue off, but she let the inference slide, said,

"Young people have neither the time nor inclination for such refinement."

I said,

"More's the Irish pity."

I let the envelope lie, said,

"Let's defer that until I achieve the target."

"Will you attend the Month's Minds Mass?"

My God, a month already since Sheila Winston had been murdered. I delayed, asked,

"Where is the Mass?"

"Sheila loved the Abbey so that will be the official venue. We, of course, will have a private ceremony here."

I pushed, asked,

"Am I invited to that?"

She sighed.

"You really do test a person. This is an enclosed convent, as you well know."

I was on a roll, said,

"But I'm on the payroll, kind of."

She stood up, dismissal time.

"Thank you for yet again agreeing to help us."

I said,

"A nun in need is indeed?"

"Goodbye, Mr. Taylor."

The little nun who let me out the front door said,

"Mother Superior does like you."

I asked,

"What's not to like?"

Outside the convent, the heat rose from the pavement like a clerical assault, fast and brutal. I walked along the canals, and a guy was fishing down near the Róisín Dubh. He greeted me,

"Taylor, heard you were dead."

This was a familiar greeting to me and the years I'd been comatose only added to the belief. I asked,

"Catching anything?"

He answered,

"You know how many years I've been fishing from this exact spot?"

The fuck would I know, or care? I said,

"How would I know that?"

He spun around, snapped,

"No need to be snarky."

This was truly one of those conversations going nowhere so I said,

"I'll leave you to it."

He waited until I was past him, then,

"Liked you better when I thought you were dead."

Irish logic at its shining best.

It was believed for a long time

   That

      Nuns in an enclosed order

         Were

            Secretive until

               A bishop in the north of Ireland declared

                  They were

                     Confidential.

30

Salman Rushdie was attacked at a literary event in New York and stabbed seventeen times. Somehow, he survived, though the diagnosis was kidney and liver damage and maybe the loss of an eye. His assailant was a young man with no apparent ties to terrorist groups.

J. K. Rowling posted her shock and sympathy on Twitter and almost immediately a post appeared, threatening,

"You're next."

The FBI raided the Florida home of Trump and removed boxes of documents from there. Trump, of course, expressed his outrage and his supporters vowed to reelect him in 2024.

In Ireland, the number of refugees from Ukraine hit the seventy thousand mark and little or no accommodation was available.

I continued to search for Raftery to no avail. Quinlan assured me that he would find him.

The heat wave had lasted for ten days, and the population was struck near speechless from sunburn. A day of heavy rain, thunder, lightning was almost a relief.

I went to the movies.

Jordan Peele had written, produced two major horror movies in the previous years: *Get Out*

And

Us.

So it was with much anticipation I went to see his third production, titled *Nope.*

And a major disappointment it was too.

Spending two hours at the cinema carried its own brand of guilt.

I resolved to double down on the effort to locate Raftery.

At the cinema, when I asked for a ticket to the movie, I was told,

"We don't accept cash."

What the fuck?

I asked,

"How am I supposed to get a ticket?"

The ticket guy could give a shit, said,

"Swipe card."

I was livid.

Eventually, I used my credit card and asked the guy,

"What if you don't have a credit card?"

He gave me a look like I was a complete ejit.

"Then you don't get to see the movie."

More and more, the cashless society was imposing its will, and older people were truly a new kind of poor. I remembered when the churches installed electronic candles and the whole beautiful ritual of getting a taper, lighting it, and the smell of wax as you lit the candle was gone.

The whole fabric of how we lived was changed but not improved.

Another nun was attacked, seriously injured, and my guilt hit DEFCON five.

The Mother Superior left me a stack of messages but I didn't answer.

What could I say?

Sorry?

August had been a blistering month in every sense and the hope of September was the top of a prayer list.

The nuclear facility in Ukraine was teetering on the edge of leaking. The technicians were Ukraine, but the facility was Russian held. Echoes of Chernobyl were rife.

I walked the dog.

We started at Blackrock Pier, at the end of the Salthill Promenade, kicked the wall as is the Galway tradition and headed in the direction of town. The distance was estimated at about three kilometers so there and back would yield a six-kilometer hike.

Outside Seapoint Ballroom a guy stopped in front of us, asked,

"Jack Taylor?"

I said,

"Yeah."

I held a tight grip on the dog's leash as my instinct whispered,

"This guy is off."

He said,

"You don't remember me?'

I said,

"Nope."

Sounding a little like the movie.

He moved closer.

"I used to drink in The Quays, and you got me barred."

The fuck was this guy?

I said the only thing I could, said,

"You're kidding, I don't drink in The Quays, and if I did, getting someone barred is, like, just about the last thing I'd do. I can safely say you are a total stranger to me."

The dog gave a low growl, picking up on the vibe. The guy said,

"I forgive you."

I gave a short bitter laugh, snarled,

"Don't forgive me, and you know what? If they barred you, they were right. Now fuck off."

He shook his head, a tolerant smile on his face. He said,

"You're a bitter, angry man. No wonder you drink so much."

I brushed past him, the dog reluctant to end the gig so fast.

Ahead of me was a van with the logo:

Mike Denver and Band

There was a list of dates for the concerts on the back window. If I were the dancing kind, and perish the thought if I were, I'd have gone to see Mike. He was one of the good guys.

I looked back at where I'd met the guy who forgave me.

I said to Trip,

"Do I look forgiven?"

Down through Shop Street and the buskers were out in style. Every musical instrument was on show:

Bodhran.

Spoons.

Melodeons.

Guitars.

Fiddles.

Improvised drums, i.e.,

biscuit tins inverted.

I thought Trip might be disturbed by the cacophony of sounds, but I was beginning to realize he was a calm canine. Good that one of us wasn't overly disturbed.

Outside Dubray bookshop, a woman asserted,

"You're Jack Taylor."

Indeed.

She looked at the dog, said,

"I thought at the very least you'd have a Rottweiler."

I answered,

"These dogs were used by Chinese emperors to fight lions."

"It's a long time since those dogs fought anythin'."

"You obviously haven't been drinking in the city pubs."

I was tying Trip to a railing outside Charlie Byrne's bookstore when Vinny appeared. He said,

"You have a new dog?"

Where to start? Maybe just give the bold truth. I said,

"A nun bequeathed him to me."

And yes, that sentence does sound as odd as it looks. It had a whirl-wind of questions therein.

"A nun?"

"Why?"

"To you, really?"

"And why are you tying the poor creature to the railing? Are you tired of him already?"

But Vinny has run a bookshop in Galway, along with Charlie Byrne's, for forty years so eccentric behavior is nothing remarkable, indeed it's downright near mandatory.

I went for the brief version, said,

"I was friends with a nun, she died and willed the dog to me."

Vinny took this in stride, said,

"Bring him, somebody might steal him."

True enough, pedigree dogs were being snatched all over the city.

Noirin was inside the door, she went nuts for Trip, picked him up and disappeared into the children's department.

I asked Vinny,

"Will she come back?"

"Probably not."

I reckon if I could have lived in a bookstore, my life would have been a dream. But the devil had other plans.

Outside of Charlie's, a guy asked me for a loan of a tenner. I gave him five and he said,

"That makes me half-grateful."

The dog didn't like him much either.

※

We got back to the flat and I set out a bowl of kibble for Trip. He loved
the stuff, especially if I sprinkled some chicken bits in there.

I poured myself a large Jameson, and drained that sucker in one.
The bizarre day I'd had, who could blame me.

There was an envelope on the carpet, my name on it. I recognized
Mother Superior's distinctive script.

I opened it and a slim book fell out.

The Art of War

Inside the cover she'd written,

"Bring the war to him."

※

Liz Truss becomes the UK prime minister. Bad news for the Northern
Ireland Protocol. Neither Sinn Féin nor the Orange Order welcome
her victory.

She faces an avalanche of problems.

Ukraine.

Refugees.

Galloping inflation.

Not to mention a fractured Tory party with mumblings of Johnson
in the wings in the wild hope of a return to power.

I told all this to the dog, who promptly went to sleep.

I read about the small metal capsules I'd noticed scattered on the streets.

Nitrous oxide.

The newest fad for the young, who opted for this craze instead of booze.

The medical profession already warning of brain damage and other serious side effects. Smoking seemed to pretty much be fully on the way out as vaping spread among the young.

In Tallaght in Dublin, twins, aged eight, their sister, eighteen, were stabbed to death by their twenty-four-year-old brother.

In Canada, two brothers went on a killing spree, knifed ten people to death, injuring eighteen others.

I sat back, trying to figure what would calm my mind amid the frenzy.

Nitrous oxide?

Vaping?

Settled for a plain shot of Jameson, large. The devil you know.

"Security against defeat
Implies
Defensive tactics.
Ability to defeat the enemy
Means
Taking the offensive."

                    —Sun Tzu
                The Art of War

31

I had photos of Raftery on my phone, so I downloaded a stack of those, put my mobile number on the back, and added that a hefty reward was available for any information. When all else fails, put the cash out there.

The Queen died and Prince Charles is the new king.

A ninety-six-gun salute was performed as tribute to the longevity of her reign, the longest serving monarch. When she'd come to Ireland, she seemed to instinctively know how to reach the people. Chatting to a fishmonger in Cork market, giving a speech that began in Irish.

Class.

I walked the dog in Berna woods and his joy in pursuing leaves, then rolling and wallowing in the shrubbery, made my heart soar. In my befuddled and bewildering career, I had briefly the care of a peregrine falcon, and how that bird would fly, that feeling with the dog was reminiscent of it. A short window of near happiness.

Raftery
Was
Found.

32

It was late in the evening. I'd made Irish stew, not like my mother made it. I put:

Carrots,

Onions,

Gravy,

Mass of spuds.

And as this came to a nice boil, I added shots of Jameson. I piled it on a plate, put some in the dog's dish, cracked a long neck, put on *Better Call Saul*, and tucked in.

This is not by any means a definition of contentment, but it was lurking in that elusive neighborhood. I'd just finished and was debating a cig when the doorbell went. The dog barked, as if he was pissed our evening idyll was interrupted.

I opened the door to Father Pat, who seemed sober. He was dressed in mid-cleric garb, blue jeans but black sweater and the white collar. A mixed message indeed. He asked,

"Something smells good?"

I waved him in, and he literally jumped when he saw the dog, said,

"That's a dog."

Before I could snarl, he ventured,

"I'm a cat person."

Like I gave a flying fuck.

"Want some dinner?"

He looked to the large pot on the range.

"If I'm not intruding."

I fixed him a bowl, asked,

"To drink?"

Testing his new earned sobriety?

He asked for a glass of milk.

He ate with relish, then suddenly stopped, sat back as if scalded, roared,

"There's booze in this."

So?

I said with a measured tone,

"It's Irish stew. The clue is in the name, Irish."

He stood up, rage writ large, accused,

"You deliberately tried to sabotage me."

I said,

"You had a taste, nothing more, don't sweat it."

He shook his head, near spat,

"You're a bad person. I mean, I know that, but I thought you'd have more consideration for your friends."

I said,

"We're not friends. I mean, seriously, who has priest friends?"

He reached in his jacket, pulled out a sheet of paper, slapped it on the table. It was the printout I'd had made up, of Raftery. I asked,

"You know where he is?"

He glared at me, sneered,

"I've a good mind not to tell you."

"Then when he attacks another nun, it will be on you."

He seemed to struggle with this, then,

"He came to me in confession."

Fuck.

Would we be breaking the seal of that ritual?

He read my mind, answered,

"He didn't come for confession; he came for confrontation."

Oh.

I echoed,

"Confrontation?"

He sighed, said,

"He had your leaflet in his hand, said to tell you it would take more than a f— piece of paper to bother him."

I asked,

"What did you say?"

He gave a small smile, said,

"I asked him not to curse in the confessional."

I waited, then asked,

"What happened after?"

Pat said,

"He stormed out, kicked the box."

"And what did you do?"

"I followed him."

I was so delighted I nearly hugged him, but hugging a priest?

Yeah.

I said,

"That is great. Where did he go?"

Pat was well pleased with himself. He took his time, then,

"There's a house for refugees off Sheridan's pub, on the right side of the docks, number seventeen, Raglan Road. With the number of people milling about, it's perfect cover for hiding in plain sight."

I admitted,

"You did good."

He was pleased, asked,

"When will the Guards be alerted?"

"No Guards."

He protested,

"You must call them, what? You think you can take him on your own?"

I said,

"I'll have help."

He wasn't satisfied.

"I'm not convinced; you probably mean your hurly."

He was right, I would bring that, but I also would call Quinlan.

Pat, as he headed for the door, asked,

"You won't do vigilante stuff?"

I gave him my best smile.

Quinlan arrived at my apartment, dressed for a hunt.

Black combat trousers, black T, black plimsolls, black windbreaker.

I said,

"Black is the new vengeance."

He had a holdall that he laid gingerly on the floor. I looked at him, asked,

"Is that incendiary?"

He gave me a tight smile.

"It's not sandwiches."

"You have a plan?"

And he laughed, said,

"It's Raftery, plans are redundant."

I got my rucksack, put the hurly in, put on my all-weather Garda coat. The weather had turned cold in the second week of Sept. Quinlan glanced at the Jameson bottle, said,

"We'll have a drink after."

After what? I wondered, but kept that thought to myself.

We got to the house in early evening, and it was a-buzz with activity. A mass of people milling about but there was an air of desperation over everything. Quinlan nodded to three men off to the right, said,

"They're Ukraine."

I didn't know how he could tell as there were so many nationalities gathered. I asked,

"How can you tell?"

He gave a bitter sigh, said,

"They seem to have a look of hope."

Jesus.

I said,

"Fuck, that's cynical."

He shrugged, said,

"Naw, just Ireland today."

We pushed our way inside, found what appeared to be some sort of reception desk with a tall thin man sorting through reams of paper, and were pointedly ignored. Quinlan slapped his large right hand hard on the papers, said,

"Bit of manners, eh."

The man had a name tag:

Albert.

He seemed for a short moment to consider removing Quinlan's hand, but something whispered to him,

Careful.

He let out a harried breath, asked,

"What can I help you with . . ."

Pause.

"Gentlemen?"

I gave Albert my most focused stare, the one that suggests shite is coming down their pike. I asked,

"A man using the name Raftery, or maybe not?"

I gave a description of him.

And Albert said,

"The top-floor suites."

Suites!

We turned to leave, when Albert interjected,

"But he's gone now."

Fuck.

Albert continued,

"He left with the priest."

Double fuck.

I asked,

"What priest?"

Albert got more than a little joy in answering,

"The young priest who came to warn him that men from Immigration would be coming."

I described the priest and Albert nodded. I said to Quinlan,

"Father Pat."

Albert seemed to enjoy seeing us thwarted, he had a smug smile as he added,

"That photo you have of Mr. Raftery is not quite accurate."

Quinlan scoffed,

"Little of our Raftery information seems accurate."

The anger in his voice was lethal.

I asked,

"What's the difference?"

"He's bald."

Quinlan guffawed, said,

"Of course he is."

"Might you have an idea where they might have gone?"

Albert looked at me like I was not fully with the game, said,

"To the church."

Saint Patrick's church was the church of my childhood. It was no longer in use as a brash, ugly new building was erected beside it. It was big, it was spacious, and Mass on a Sunday highlighted the empty seats. In the small old church, I remembered it jammed with people.

The church had power then.

Those days went the way of old-fashioned candles. Now they were electronic, push a button, miss a prayer. You could attend Mass on Zoom, killing the communal spirit that once permeated the parish.

The government was in a serious panic over refugees and yet empty churches remained empty.

I said to Quinlan,

"If Pat is still sheltering him, he'll use the old church."

The front door was boarded up, but you could tell it had recently been opened and then the boards hastily restored.

Quinlan asked,

"Is there another door?'

I snapped,

"What am I? The ecclesiastical planner? I have no idea."

We got the door opened but it creaked like a very ancient sermon.

It was dark and we took a moment to get our bearings. Gradually, a figure was visible in the front pew. I moved slowly up the aisle, the hurly gripped tight. The figure was a man, and he was slumped over the rail.

It was Pat.

His neck was broken.

"You know it's summer
In Ireland
When
The rain gets warmer."
—Hal Roach

33

We had rain of a biblical nature.

I was watching Sky News. The line to pass the coffin of the Queen, who was lying in state, had people standing for twenty-four hours. King Charles the Third, in his first official act, sacked three hundred staff from his former residence, Clarence House. He had stated that he intended to slim down the Crown.

As Ukraine continued to regain territory and the Russians were pushed farther north, Putin warned that he would use every weapon at his disposal.

The nuclear threat was very clear and chilling.

My phone rang. I didn't recognize the number, answered,

"Yeah?"

"Mr. Taylor, this is Albert from the refugee center."

"Oh right, what can I do for you?"

He paused, then,

"I have information I think is of deep significance for you."

"Oh, okay."

Another pause, then he said,

"This is where you make an offer."

I asked,

"You want paying?"

He gave a short laugh.

"Inflation is through the roof, Mr. Taylor; we all have to pay."

When I didn't respond, he said,

"I'll be in Monroe's pub in an hour. If you don't show, I'll sell it to the next in line."

He hung up.

I gathered up the cash I had, put it in my all-weather coat, dressed for a shakedown, i.e., darkly.

Said to the dog,

"You mind the house; I'll mind our business."

Monroe's, along with the Róisín Dubh, provides some of the best music in the city and is a lively, hopping venue. I walked down Dominic Street and ran into Robin and his son Chris. Stalwarts of the showband era, it is a lift to the spirit to hear them as enthusiastic now as Robin was in his heyday of the dance halls.

They offered to buy me a drink, but I said,

"I have to meet a guy for a spot of extortion."

They took that in their stride, they knew me well enough to get that I might be serious.

We agreed we'd meet up soon and I watched them walk away. I felt a pang of regret for all that the showband era had signified and how nothing had ever replaced it.

Monroe's was busy but it was one of those pubs that always was. Albert was lurking near the big window, furtiveness enshrouding him. He had a pint glass in his hand, near empty. He said,

"Get the drinks in then."

Turns out I knew the barman. When you know a lot of barmen, your life is not much of a mystery. I got two pints, and brought them back to Albert, handed him one. He said,

"Some Jameson would have been welcome."

I ignored that.

And waited.

He said,

"I'll need paying."

I gave him a short smile, waited.

He caved first, said,

"Your friend, the hard-ass who was with you, he'd been before."

What?

I tried to hide my shock, asked,

"What did he want?"

Albert sat back, smiled, said,

"That's the second part of the information. I'll need paying for the first before we continue."

I got my wallet, pulled out two fifties, laid them on the table. He sneered,

"Worth more than that."

Now I smiled, took one fifty back, said,

"Clock is ticking."

He grabbed the remaining note, said,

"He wanted to know about Raftery, I told him about the priest."

Jesus wept.

I finished my pint, moved to leave, and Albert asked,

"Fancy another pint?"

"I would, just not with you."

I took Trip for a walk, out along The Claddagh Road, leading to Grattan Road, and we jumped down to the beach there. I let Trip off the leash and appreciated his joy in running free along the wide stretch of sand. It spurred my heart to see him fly.

There were other dog walkers about, and they greeted me warmly. A fine-looking lady, dressed in a Barbour jacket, red Wellingtons that had faded jeans tucked into them. Her hair was blond, thick, and blowing alluringly in the wind. If I squinted my eyes, it could have been a commercial for Clairol.

She spoke,

"Is the *tizz su* [*sic*] your dog?"

I agreed it was. Her dog was a Staffordshire mix and just about the ugliest creature you could imagine, his teeth protruded, giving a jolly-thug slant to his face. She gave a short laugh as I stared at him, said,

"Isn't he one ugly little fellah?"

"I'm not sure about the little."

I said,

"I'm Jack Taylor."

Put out my hand. She took it in hers, nice firm grip, said,

"Rachel Worthington."

She had one of those strong faces that American women specialize in. Her accent had a hint of Boston, overlaid with some, what was the English term, received English, as if it arrived in the mail.

She was smiling and I asked,

"What?"

She said,

"No offense but you seem like you should have a bigger dog."

"Oh, don't let him hear you say that, he's touchy about his size."

She laughed.

"How very male of him."

We walked along the beach as the dogs chased in and out of the surf. Rachel asked,

"Are you a wild swimmer?"

"I've been wild at times, for sure, but not in the water."

Wild swimming had increased massively in the previous two years. I'd resisted any temptation to follow them.

Her dog approached and she put his leash on, asked,

"Are you going to offer me a drink sometime?"

I asked,

"Will I have to go swimming?"

"No."

She said,

"Just wild."

We arranged to meet in Garavan's at seven the following evening. She added as she strode away,

"Dress as if you're excited."

Damn. The thing was, I did feel the touch of that. The dog looked at me, shook himself dry from the water, and wet me thoroughly, cooling me, so to speak.

We were heading for McCambridge's when a woman stopped me outside Eason, said,

"McCambridge's has been sold."

Another Galway institution bites the dust. At Christmas, they made up hampers that were a joy to receive. Vinny from Charlie Byrne's bookstore was standing at Powell's corner. I asked him,

"Don't tell me you guys are selling up?"

He gave a rueful smile, said,

"Nope."

34

The Galleon restaurant in Salthill is one of the oldest in the city and has served over a million people in its time. The owner, Ger, was as down to earth as it gets. She greeted me warmly and I introduced her to Rachel.

She seemed to click instantly with Rachel, said to her,

"Jack has been coming here for years and always orders the same thing."

Rachel gave me a fond look, said,

"Consistency is to be valued."

I liked her more already.

Ger gave us the window table; we ordered a glass of wine for Rachel and a pint for me. When the waitress came with menus, Rachel said,

"I'll have the Jack usual."

This consisted of:

Sausages.

Mashed spuds.

Onions, fried and mixed in the potato.

And lashings of gravy.

Heaven.

Rachel raised her glass, tried,

"Sláinte."

"Sláinte amach" (means *back at ya*).

I said,

"Good pronunciation!"

We were on a second drink when the food came, and Rachel gasped, went,

"That's a lot of food."

"Why I come here."

Rachel ate like a good un, and clearly enjoyed the food, I was relieved.

On finishing, she said,

"I met your brother today."

You think you reach a certain age and nothing can surprise you, but I was shocked to my core. I managed a feeble,

"What?"

She said,

"I was on my way home and this good-looking man stopped me, said he was your brother and gave me an envelope for you."

She rooted in her bag, pulled out a white envelope, written on it was,

"The late Jack Taylor."

She said,

"I think the late must be some sort of code between you?"

Where to begin and what to tell her?

I opened the envelope and a black sheet of paper filtered out. Silver writing said,

> Jack, I didn't kill the priest, I'm still in nun mode. I like
> this new lady of yours, and I won't kill her yet.
>
> Just kidding. Lighten up, bro.
>
> On a more serious level, stop searching for me. It's very
> annoying, and I'd hate to wipe you off the board when you
> just finally found a woman, so back off, big guy,
>
> Your brother in matters ecclesiastical.
>
> Raftery.

Rachel leaned over, put her hand on mine, asked,

"Is everything okay?"

Where to begin?

As my mind whirled round trying to find a point of entry to the whole sorry saga, my overwhelming feeling was sorrow that I'd have to end whatever budding relationship I might have with Rachel as Raftery was already threatening her.

I asked,

"Where did you meet him?"

Her face now held the beginning of anxiety. She said,

"I was walking the dog in Eyre Square and he just walked up to me. He was very gracious, very polite, and I didn't get any sense of oddness about him."

I called Ger for the bill, to Rachel's surprise. She asked,

"No dessert?"

I snapped,

"No."

It came out like a lash. She reeled back as if I'd struck her. Ger was concerned, asked,

"Was everything all right?"

"Fine," I said.

We got outside and I stood for a moment, wondering if Raftery was nearby. I hailed a cab, held the door for Rachel, and closed it. She was astonished, asked,

"Are you not coming?"

"No," I said.

And walked away.

In Galway, when
You are taken into someone's
Confidence, the implication
Is
That up until now
You weren't
To be trusted.

35

Father Pat's funeral was a dismal affair. A small turnout.

Officiating priest, a Guard, two forlorn people who could only be his parents . . .

And me. The priest droned on about man being full of misery and other dire descriptions.

When it was done, the man spoke, said,

"There will be refreshments in Tonerys, and all are welcome."

All hung in the air like the worst kind of broken promise.

I went.

At the bar were the couple, staring into glasses of whiskey. I did consider running. But the man spotted me, signaled me to approach, shook my hand, thanked me for attending. His wife looked devastated. He asked,

"Are you a priest?"

Good God.

"No, I am . . . was a friend of your son."

The woman touched my arm, said,

"Thanks for being his friend."

Fuck.

I tried,

"He was a fine young man and I'm sure as a priest he was terrific."

They both looked at me as if I was kidding. They said in unison,

"But he was a dipsomaniac."

Wow.

I felt a tinge of anger.

"He got sober."

And the father near shouted,

"But he got killed, sober people don't get killed."

If only.

We stood in awkward silence for a solid five minutes and the father examined me closely, asked,

"What do you do?"

Whoops.

"I'm in the security business."

God on a bike, why did I say that?

The man looked dubious, said,

"I'm in real estate."

And we descended into more silence until the man asked,

"You want to buy a house?"

I said,

"Let me buy you a drink."

He waved his hands.

"It's a free bar, for the funeral and all."

As we were all of three mourners, we had a wide range. I accepted another Jameson and the woman asked,

"Are you fond of it yourself, the drink, I mean?"

Phew-oh.

I think sweat had broken out on my forehead. I said,

"'Tis a comfort in times like this."

Not to mention a bloody dire necessity.

The man said,

"We'll have a sit-down meal after. You are invited to join us."

Not if hell froze over.

"Very good of you to ask me but I have a prior engagement."

The man considered this, accused,

"Something more important than honoring my dead son?"

I finished my drink, put out my hand,

"Again, my deepest sympathy."

The man asked,

"When will the rest of the mourners appear?"

The fuck!

I lied, looked at my watch, said,

"Any minute now."

And got out of there.

On the path were two ne'er-do-wells looking thirsty, broke, and desperate. I said to them,

"Go into the bar, there's a couple at the counter. Sympathize over their dead son and you can drink for free."

They liked the concept. One of them asked,

"What did the son do? You know, so we can wing it."

"He was a priest."

One spoke,

"I'm not fond of priests."

My agitation rising, I near shouted,

"Someone killed the poor bastard."

They mulled over that, then one asked,

"Who'd kill a priest?"

When I got back to my apartment, Quinlan was waiting outside. Dressed in a dark tracksuit, he had a rucksack at his feet. He greeted,

"Jack, where have you been?"

Rage simmered, danced on the outskirts of my heart. I strove for a civil tone, said,

"I was at the funeral of a priest, you may remember him, Father Pat?"

His face did a fine job of feigning mild shock.

"That is a shame. I can't say I'm too fond of the man since he took it on himself to warn Raftery."

I opened the door to my apartment, moved to the side, motioned to him to follow, and as he did so, I gripped the side of the door, slammed it full wallop into his face. He crashed back against the corridor wall, I followed, kicked him in the balls. He went down like a lost petition.

I pulled him by his collar into the apartment, tied him to a chair, tied him tight, waited.

He gradually came to, spat remnants of teeth and blood on the carpet, muttered,

"The fuck is with you, Jack?"

I said,

"You killed that young priest, you figured I'd blame Raftery."

He shook his head, spat,

"He betrayed us."

He managed a bitter smile, asked,

"What now, Jack, you going to kill me?"

"No," I said.

He waited and I added,

"I'm going to do something I've never done."

He sneered,

"What's that then?"

"Call the Guards."

And I did.

They arrested me,

    For false imprisonment,

        Assault and battery.

In the interview room at the station, I told them my story.

Quinlan was in a room down the hall. I was allowed a phone call and used it to contact Brown, my previous solicitor. I chose him because he'd been a vociferous critic of the Guards in the past months, and he knew me.

He arrived shortly after the call, had a brief word with me, then headed for the Superintendent's office. An hour later I was out on bail.

I asked him,

"How did you achieve that?"

He was a big man, ruddy face and a head of hair that would never submit to a comb. Energy oozed from him like the best form of hope. He gave a laugh, said,

"DNA, from the priest's clothes to items in Quinlan's rucksack, I guaranteed them there would be a match when it was tested. It was sufficient to raise doubt on your case."

While I considered that, he added,

"Doesn't hurt that I play golf with the commissioner."

I asked,

"But aren't you currently at war with the Guards?"

He shrugged that away with,

"Ah, that's just work. Golf is important."

In Galway

 It is believed

  That when someone

   Takes you into

    Their confidence

   It is

    To gag you.

36

The country in deep mourning after a terrible accident. In Donegal, a petrol station in the center of a small town exploded, ten people were killed.

Each day saw one of the funerals pass through the town. It united the country, North and South, in a way not seen for a decade.

In Ukraine, Putin's symbolic new bridge linking Crimea was destroyed by Ukraine forces. It was a fresh humiliation for Putin, who was running low on troops, supplies, and his country short on food. He threatened even closer to nuclear options.

Inflation was running at an all-time high, and people were unable to pay the huge new gas and fuel bills. A government minister suggested the population wear vests! The church whined that they were unable to heat the churches and that shorter Masses would be introduced, and the congregation could wear those vests.

A whistleblower reveals that for more than thirty years, Irish dancing competitions for young girls have been fixed. The country truly let out a collective gasp of . . .

Is nothing, nothing f— sacred?

Nope.

I took the dog for a long walk, through the Spanish Arch then up to the Wolfe Tone bridge, the spot where I'd been stabbed. I turned toward The Claddagh Church, moving along the quay where the swans gathered. The dog stopped and gazed in wonder at the birds. The swans took no notice of him, dogs were of no advantage in their existence.

An old fisherman sitting on the quay bench watched me, asked,

"What kind of mutt is that?"

I told him and he made a sound that was not approving. He said,

"There was a time, people got some color of mongrel and paid little heed to it. Now they are buying coats for them."

As I walked away, he shouted,

"Get a real dog for fucksakes!"

I walked along by the Connemara Road until I reached Grattan Road. And a joy to let the dog off the leash and fly across the beach. There was a strong wind, and it took me a moment to realize my name was being called.

Rachel, with her dog.

She looked terrific, wearing one of those Belle crew weather jackets. In the distance, they look like leather. She had faded blue jeans tucked into suede boots.

She made me feel shabby.

She asked,

"How are you, Jack?"

I spoke,

"I feel shabby."

She laughed, replied,

"You sure behaved shabby."

I figured I might go for the truth, see where it led.

I said,

"The man who approached you, said he was my brother, he's a stone-cold psycho, he has been attacking nuns and he has threatened to harm you. I thought if I cut off contact with you, it might keep you safe."

She listened intently and didn't seem unduly alarmed, she reached in her bag, took out a silver flask, said,

"Call this a Jack Taylor move."

And she offered me the flask. I took it, drank deep, and phew-oh, it nigh knocked me on my arse. I asked,

"The hell is that?"

She took a drink herself and seemed to take it without effect. She said,

"It's a concoction my father used to make, so I'm continuing a tradition."

I looked out at the ocean; the dogs were having a high old time in the surf.

She was quiet for a time, then asked,

"Have you heard of Edge?"

I asked,

"Like the guitarist in U2?"

Then I added,

"Two or three times I have heard it, one of those urban myths that do the rounds."

I vaguely recalled talk of a vigilante crew, and the lawyer Brown had mentioned them, but the stories were always shrouded in rumor and innuendo. Even the Mother Superior had dismissed them.

Trip came running up the beach, shook himself at my feet, and covered me in sea spray.

Rachel took another swig from the flask, began,

"Edge is a group of people who term themselves the last resort. When justice has failed or is unable to act for some reason, Edge steps in. But, and it's a huge *but*, they must be asked. In return, they demand a favor in the future."

I asked,

"Who are they?"

She took a deep breath then, said,

"Doctors,

"Guards,

"Politicians,

"Citizens,

"Soldiers."

Her dog came bounding across the sand and she greeted him like she'd never seen him before. I liked that, a lot.

She said,

"People who've reached the end of their patience with the justice system and are literally crying out for help, Edge steps in."

She took a deep breath and her dog folded itself into her as if sensing her disturbance. She continued,

"My son, Conor, seventeen years old, was killed by a drunk driver, a man named Trenton, who was driving an Audi. He hit my son so hard that my boy's body was almost in two."

She stopped, produced the flask, and drank deep, handed it to me, said,

"I'm sorry, I'm usually more in control. Trenton was given a suspended sentence and community service. He still drank . . ."

Pause.

"And drove."

She composed herself.

"A man approached me, said he could help deliver justice for me, and sometime later, I might provide a small service for his organization, named Edge. I agreed instantly. I was insane with grief; I'd have agreed to anything if it eased the anguish."

She continued,

"A month after, Trenton was found hanging in Barna woods, the keys to a new Audi at his dangling feet."

The dogs were flat out, knackered from their play. I felt knackered my own self.

We sat in silence until I asked,

"Did they ask you for a favor?"

"Yes."

I waited.

She shook herself as if rearranging her bearing. She said,

"They asked me to contact you."

The
    Fields
        Of
           Athenry

37

I agreed that I would be available to perform a favor for Edge if they helped catch Raftery. Rachel emphasized that they would ask for something and it would not be negotiable. I said I was fine with that.

A week later, I got a call to wait outside my building, and was told,

"Bring your hurly."

I duly waited and a van arrived, two men in it. Brief nods were exchanged, no words. We drove to Athenry, stopped before a large farmhouse, the driver indicated for me to get out. A man came out of the farmhouse, he surveyed me, said,

"I'm Tarry Flynn, like the Patrick Kavanagh story."

He looked at the hurly in my rucksack, said,

"You came prepared, good. Let's go see the livestock."

He led me to a large barn, and I followed him in. Raftery was tied to a hard chair, his left eye heavily bruised but otherwise seemed unharmed. He exclaimed,

"Jack fucking Taylor, Christ, you never give up."

I moved up close to him and he jeered at me.

"What now, wise guy, you going to beat me with your hurly?"

I had a hundred things I intended to say to him, but my mind was just ice cold. I felt the slow solid beat of rage.

Flynn said,

"I'll leave you to him."

I stared at Raftery, then I swung the hurly with all the ferocity in my heart.

I was in the hospital, sitting by the bed of a man in a coma.

Raftery.

The nurse who had attended me was amazed, said,

"Your brother sat by you and now here you are doing the same for him, 'tis a wonder."

Indeed.

I went every day. I wanted to be there when he came to.

On a Saturday evening, I had just washed the dog, who was now sulking. I poured a large Jay, gave the dog a mash-up of nuts with chicken pieces. I think he forgave me a bit.